Good Girls
Don't Wear Trousers

Good Girls
Don't Wear Trousers

LARA CARDELLA

Translated from the Italian by
Diana Di Carcaci

Arcade Publishing • New York

FIRST U.S. EDITION 1994

Originally published in Italy under the title *Volevo i Pantaloni*

The characters and events in this book are fictitious. Any similarity to
real persons, living or dead, is coincidental and not intended by the
author.

Library of Congress Cataloging-in-Publication Data

Cardella, Lara, 1969–
    [Volevo i pantaloni. English]
    Good girls don't wear trousers / Lara Cardella : translated by
Diana Di Carcaci. — 1st U.S. ed.
      p.   cm.
    ISBN 1-55970-263-X
    1. Girls — Italy — Sicily — Fiction.   2. Sicily (Italy) — Social
life and customs — Fiction.   I. Di Carcaci, Diana.   II. Title.
PQ4863.A69375V6513   1993
853'.914 — dc20   94-14354

Published in the United States by Arcade Publishing, Inc., New York
Distributed by Little, Brown and Company

10 9 8 7 6 5 4 3 2 1

BP

Designed by API

PRINTED IN THE UNITED STATES OF AMERICA

Good Girls
Don't Wear Trousers

I never dreamed about marrying Prince Charming. Where I come from, either you dreamed about him or about the heavenly father, or you didn't dream at all. I had dreamed about our heavenly father ever since, at the age of five, I had been informed that the person up in the sky with the beard and rolling eyes and commanding forefinger was my father. I never loved my father on earth because he refused to let me wear trousers and told me I must never let people see my legs. However, I had hopes that the father in the sky would see to it that one of these days I would be able to wear trousers like my brother, and show my legs like Angelina, engineer Carasotti's daughter. Sprawled on the bed in my room, I made drawings of God in which, instead of pointing majestically, his finger would be folded into my tiny fist, which curled around it tightly and lovingly. Then Dad would come in, see what I was doing, and announce that I would burn in hell, my drawings were so blasphemous. He couldn't grasp the simple fact that I loved God.

So, as I embarked on adolescence, I opted for the convent. I was in secondary school, achieving less than dazzling results and being a great disappointment to everyone. During tedious hours of Latin I would gaze out of the window and imagine that God was watching over me, and from time to time I would find myself smiling involuntarily. School wasn't really a free choice: my father had imposed a drastic alternative ("It's either school for you, my girl, or you stay at home and help your mother"), and I decided that I preferred the classroom to staying at home bent over a loom or slaving for hours over gallons of tomato sauce. I wasn't cut out for domesticity, still less for the classics; perhaps I wasn't cut out for anything, but I had to do something, if only to prove that I had no intention of being supported by a boy from "a good family."

As I mentioned, this was the time when I longed to go into a convent. I lost myself in the thoughts of the religious, cloistered life, and whenever I saw a nun it was all I could do to restrain myself from lifting the skirts of her habit to ascertain whether she wore trousers underneath. I seldom went to mass though, because, with the best will in the world, it was impossible to stay awake during Father Domenico's interminable sermons. I was convinced that my faith was very pure and spiritual and that my relationship with God had to be kept within the four walls of my bedroom so that I wouldn't have to share him with anyone else; I had him all to myself. It goes without saying that this approach to religion didn't cut much ice with the locals. If they had any notion of a relationship with God, it was something so ritualized and formal that it could only be mediated by priests and by taking the sacrament on Sundays.

And my visits to confession were even more sporadic. Not that I considered myself perfect, far from it, but I couldn't bring myself to trust the sanctimonious sermons of the priests, still less their continual and pressing demands for money. I could have been scarred for life one Sunday when I witnessed Father Domenico scolding an old lady at the top of his voice for what he considered a meager contribution to the offertory plate. He assured her that such avarice had cost her her place in heaven. Quite apart from all this, I felt that I didn't need any go-between in my relationship with God since I planned soon to be his bride.

My classmates just went on dreaming about Prince Charming. They left home in the morning wearing long floral skirts and lacy white blouses, but as soon as they got to school they would congregate in the cloakroom to wield the weapons of a femme fatale. Out would come the latest glossy lipstick from Paris, the boxes of shimmering eyeshadow, and the powder compacts. They were always trying to model themselves on some famous actress, and then they'd forget which one and start bickering. They would undo their blouses and stuff their bras with Kleenex to provide more ample contours and hitch their skirts above the tops of their calf-length boots until the hems skimmed their knees. Some of the girls still wore the heavy men's shoes handed down from their mothers, who in turn had been given them by their mothers.

I would observe this transformation from a corner, gloating over the superiority of my own clothes. I always wore a navy blue pleated skirt and one of my father's long white shirts, which looked as crisp as the day it was bought and still smelled of mothballs. I laughed at the girls' attempts at seduction as they paraded down the school corridors wiggling their hips amid muffled giggles and tugs at the slipping Kleenex. The boys ogled them, and I overheard Giovanni say to Giampiero, "Look at that ass! I know what I could do with her. . . ." and "Have you seen Angelina's tits? I wouldn't mind giving her one. . . ." More obscene comments would follow as the boys' fantasies flowered, fantasies fed by the pornographic comics they had unearthed at home in the cellar, or under the bed, or in their father's box of mementos beside his pipe or his hunting hat.

Of course there was no buzz of excitement when I walked by; there would just be a deathly hush, as if no one, nothing, had passed, but this didn't bother me at all. I certainly wasn't going to waste time dreaming about Prince Charming and dolling myself up like the others. What a song and dance it was for so little admiration. To me, the boys' attitude was insulting, and anyway their comments were certainly not worth slaps and scoldings from the teachers or, worse still, from our tyrannical headmaster.

The headmaster was a throwback to the Nazis, in a version revised and perfected by himself. He admired Hitler's disciplinarianism and was, like him, convinced of his own omnipotence. He emulated these characteristics, adding Mussolini's imposing gestures for good measure. When the morning bell sounded at eight thirty, there he was at the top of the stairs, bald as a coot, puffing out his chest, and standing rigidly upright in his pressed blue suit, scanning us ferociously. He scarcely spoke a word but would make a stately descent, taking a step at a time as if savoring every one. As the girls filed past, he would eye the length of their skirts (sometimes even measuring them with a ruler) and estimate the depth of their cleavages and the transparency of their shirts as he looked over the sea of faces; eyes, mouths, and cheeks. This ritual would be repeated when the bell rang at one thirty, except that by then there would be only lingering traces of makeup and both Kleenex and skirt hems would have slipped.

On these occasions, our headmaster would explode with rage, dispensing a hail of slaps and insults. More of these would follow when, next day, he interviewed the girl, accompanied by her father. Nervously the father would interpolate, "You did right, Headmaster . . . you should have killed the little slut."

Then the mother would put the girl under house arrest and, when she did her shopping, would walk with her eyes downcast with shame. And then there'd be the usual tittle-tattle from the greengrocer and the butcher and all the other shopkeepers and the women gossiping in spiteful whispers as they watched her. "There she is. Did you ever?" It made me sick when I saw this sort of thing, but most of all I wondered why they behaved like that. After all, I had been born and brought up in the same place and in the same way, but I still couldn't fathom this insatiable desire to know everyone else's business. They knew everything about everybody; no one was spared. News spread like wildfire and was embellished at every telling: if a girl was late coming home, word went around that she had eloped, and the crash of a plate next door was a sure sign of a blazing marital quarrel, and so on. They were all the same, nosy about everybody and everything. You could say it showed the human side of the villagers, because only one thing was certain in their lives, that no one had the freedom or right to live or to die alone. In our part of the world not even a dog can die in privacy.

When one of these girls came back to school after her punishment, she was usually greeted with profound silence. But though no one uttered a sound, you could tell their minds were buzzing. They felt sorry for her but couldn't help wondering how often she had been beaten and whether that would teach her how to dress for school. Feeling the weight of all this attention, the victim would hang her head in shame, having been labeled a slut, a whore. At recess, however, the victim became a heroine, the focus of a volley of breathless questions: "What did your parents say?" "What did they beat you with? A stick?" "We heard they threw you out onto the balcony stark naked and thrashed you with a belt, you poor thing!"

Overwhelmed by questions and sympathy, the girl would choose her answers carefully so as not to antagonize anyone. Then, courage renewed, fortified by her beatings, she'd say brightly, "Pass me the lipstick, someone."

As for me, with vital statistics guaranteed never to turn heads, I stuck to my commitment as bride of Christ. This alienated me somewhat from my friends. Naturally, it did not make me greatly loved, let alone popular; the only consolation was that I was never at the top of my class, or second, which would have made me positively loathed. They looked down their noses at me (just as I did at them), considering me more or less mentally deficient, besides being negligible from a physical point of view.

Honestly, none of this bothered me. On the contrary, stoic in my halo of perfection, I was secure in the belief that I was specially chosen. My plans for a religious life and taking the veil were, gloriously, mine alone, though occasionally, overcome by an excess of spirituality, particularly in divinity classes, I was afraid that my religious fervor might show. Moments like these made it most difficult to hide my precious secret, so as an outlet I would scribble my thoughts on the cover of my notebooks, in the margins of my math exercises or my Latin translations. As you may already have gathered, I was not exactly a star pupil, though there were plenty who knew even less than I did about *ut* and the subjunctive. One girl in particular, at her wits' end, begged to copy my translation one day. My good turn was disastrous: I had forgotten to erase my scrawls about the convent and my plans to be a nun. My classmate showed remarkably little gratitude: from that day on, I was taunted by chants of "Annetta wants to be a nun, Annetta wants to be a nun," which went all around the school. Despite my stoicism this hurt, and sometimes, when I could no longer bear it, I let my halo slip and howled like a lunatic.

The worst was when my father got wind of all this, and, faced with his inquisition, I could not help but confess. He asked me how I had got the idea, and I said it was because I wanted to wear trousers. Not surprisingly, my father was a bit slow in grasping my stubborn logic, and, when I finally succeeded in explaining, all he could do was laugh. I gazed at him, mystified. Then he said, seriously this time and fixing me with a hard look, "But nuns don't wear trousers, silly, they wear habits."

A likely story, thought I, and bolted for my room, yelling that he was a liar. Luckily, I managed to lock myself in before he could take his belt to me. I lived in fear of my father and not only because of the physical pain he inflicted; he just had to look at me to fill me with terror. He had eyebrows that gave him an air of permanent rage and eyes that bored straight through me. We did not and never had gotten along. I was his daughter only when he came reluctantly forward to defend my reputation so that my chances of making a good match would not be damaged. Otherwise we barely spoke; we were light-years apart, and neither of us was prepared to budge from our fixed positions. I was just "a female," and for fathers around these parts daughters are synonymous with worry, that is until they are taken off their hands by a substitute father otherwise known as husband. Here, women can be wives and mothers but they can never be people.

Perhaps this was the reason that we hardly ever spoke to each other and that I was never able to think of the local people as friends. There was too wide a gap between being a woman and being a person, and I just wasn't able to conform. I did try to change the way I behaved but I was never able to suppress my natural high spirits, so I incurred the disapproval of everyone who felt differently. It wasn't as if I tried to change the way *they* thought; I loved them too much to be so presumptuous. There are some things so deep-rooted in us that they transcend time and space, and people who try to stifle these convictions kill the individual rather than the ideas themselves. Nonetheless there is something that thrives within us, despite the odds, and this is not your public face but your true self, your innermost being.

After I had cried for a bit, I fled the house through the window, which luckily was so near the ground that I could use it as a door. I didn't take any of my belongings, since I knew I must offer myself to God just as I was, and anyway the convent was sure to provide me with a pair of trousers and a habit.

It wasn't far, but the stifling Sicilian heat makes even doing nothing tiring. I had to go cross-country to reach the convent, and the scenery on the way was so breathtaking that the sight of it dried my tears more quickly than the sun. In Sicily the seasons do not seem to follow the usual course; it is as if time has stopped. As I made my way along the tracks and over the fields, I breathed the smell of hand-tilled soil, the trees nurtured by manure, and the sweat of men's brows. Everything here is imbued with sweat. Even the horses are never alert and frisky but are weighed down with the burden of work. Beast is indistinguishable from man and man from beast.

I arrived at the convent exhausted, after walking for well over half an hour under that sun, crying all the way. My hair was matted with sweat, and tiredness had penetrated my very bones. There loomed the great entrance portal, which I could barely see through a haze of tears, but I felt triumphant, like a martyr given up to suffering. And I was the martyr, knocking three times on the door.

A nun appeared on the balcony and looked around but, seeing nobody, went back inside. I sat on a step and fanned myself with the hem of my long skirt, licking my lips from time to time because my mouth was like a furnace. I saw her but she didn't notice me, and I stayed silent as I had no idea what to say. However, after a bit I heard chains being rattled behind me, once, twice, and finally a third time, then more rattling and the jangling of keys. I froze, tucked into a corner, trying to make myself as inconspicuous as possible. Then a face, pale as a ghost, peeked out from behind the door, looked around, and saw me.

"Whatever are you doing here?"

"Um, I . . . I want to be a nun," I stammered.

"But who are you?"

"I'm Annetta . . . my name is Anna and I'd like to become a nun," I said more resolutely.

"I see . . . but where are your parents?"

"I . . . I haven't got any. I'm an orphan and I live alone." And with that I dissolved into tears, mainly at the thought of my father's thrashing, which made me wish I really was an orphan. The nun gave me an odd look, then smiled and beckoned me in.

"All right, orphan Annie, tell me a bit about yourself."

"What . . . what do you want to know?"

"Well, you can tell me how old you are, how you have lived until now, and whether you go to school."

"I'm thirteen, and I don't go to school because I haven't got any money. . . . I used to live with my aunt Concetta, but she asked me to leave because she was so poor she couldn't feed me any longer."

"Just a minute. I thought you lived alone."

I felt myself blushing. "Oh, well, yes . . . I meant I live alone now, and since I haven't got anything to wear . . . Could I have a glass of water?"

"Of course," she said. "Wait a minute." And she disappeared inside.

I stayed where I was on that threadbare sofa, planning what to invent next and taking stock of my surroundings. There was a small hanging embroidered with the image of the Virgin Mary, an enormous crucifix that took up half the wall, two chairs, a desk, some red carnations in a vase, a large trunk, and the sofa on which I was sitting.

As soon as the nun returned with a glass of icy water, she resumed her questioning.

"So tell me, why do you want to become a nun?"

"Well, I'd like to be with God forever," I replied.

"I see, but why did you come here?"

"Because my father . . . I mean my uncle won't let me wear trousers —"

"Trousers? And what, may I ask, do they have to do with anything?" The nun was visibly amused.

"But don't you wear them under your habits? Father Domenico wears them under his cassock."

"So he should, my dear, because he's a man. No, believe me, Annetta, we don't." Then she turned away from me in a valiant attempt to suppress her laughter. I must have been a sorry sight.

"So do I have to become a priest for trousers?"

"No, you don't have to be a priest . . . but you do need to be a man. Girls don't wear trousers."

I left, utterly dejected, pursued by the nun's mirth but mulling over a whole new prospect. It was obvious that if only men could wear trousers, then, somehow, a man I must be.

With my plans for a life devoted to God in ruins, I started planning my life as a man. I was aware that it would require far more than simple willpower, no matter how determined I was. The immediate problem, however, was how to face my parents when I got home. I had been missing for over two hours, and they were bound to have noticed my absence. I thought up all sorts of excuses, but which should I use? I considered faking an accident, a broken ankle, an assault, but I knew, no matter what, that the outcome would be the same: a sound thrashing from my father. When I got back, I didn't get a chance to speak. He was waiting behind the door, belt at the ready.

"So there you are. Where the hell have you been?" he asked, the belt twitching in his hand.

Quite apart from the fact that I was in no state to produce a convincing story, there was the very real danger that one peep out of me would send him into a paroxysm of fury. I recognized all the signs that promised a beating; I had seen them too often. He looked calm, but his eyes were burning with rage. It was as if he had shifted into low gear, just waiting to give his anger full force. He reminded me of a river held in check by a wooden dam that only needs a hairline crack or the minutest weakening of one plank to burst through in a torrent, pouring forth with a ferocity increased by restraint. Once free, it knows no obstacles or hindrances. I was terrified of the potential deluge, of shifting one of the planks with a single word, a monosyllable even, so I held my breath and kept my mouth shut. It was no good: my silence only fueled his anger.

14

"What's wrong?" he shouted. "Cat got your tongue, has it?"

At that moment my mother appeared like a heavenly vision, a *dea ex machina*. I felt like Isaac, delivered from the jaws of death by the angel who, with a single gesture, averted the falling blade. My mother was an angel in a way, an angel with gray hair piled up in a bun from which wisps were constantly escaping, a barefoot angel, wearing a green-and-yellow print dress, who flung herself on me shouting, "Aha, so you've decided to come home now, have you, you little slut. . . . Where have you been?"

This was just what I was dreading: the dam was giving way, and predictably the river burst its banks. Between the thrashing and my sobs the angel could be heard wailing, egging my father on with "That's right, kill her, kill her."

With each word of encouragement, my father's strength and savagery were redoubled. He lashed at me and slapped me until I collapsed. Half-conscious, I thought I heard the angel saying, "That's enough, now. Look what you've gone and done. You've half killed her. You're a pig, that's what you are. Not even an animal deserves to be beaten like that."

And the torrent subsided, its fury sated, while the angel knelt beside me, all sweetness and maternal concern.

"Does it hurt then, poor baby? Show me. You

shouldn't take any notice of him. But promise you won't do anything like this again. Promise, you understand? Up you get now. There's nothing wrong with you."

I gave her a scornful look, picked myself up, straightened my skirt, and went to my room to ponder how to set about my latest project.

But who, or rather what, was a man? I had often heard my parents or the aunts and uncles saying, "Now, now, boys don't cry," or "Boys shouldn't play with girls," or even, "Oh, look, he'll be shaving soon." Men, I soon realized, were a race apart; coarse, strong, brave, and ruthless. I had lived what felt like a lifetime with a boy in the house and had always had to endure the burden of tradition and convention. My brother was some years older, which seemed to make him think he could be the man of the house, bossing me around, when our father was out working in the fields.

Antonio and I had never been close. I was too different, too female, for any communication to be possible, and anyway he was hardly ever at home. He usually helped Dad with his work in the fields, then came home and went straight out again. Often, he came back drunk and very late, blundering against the furniture before collapsing on his bed, still fully clothed and with his shoes on. I did not hate him; I did not hate anyone, but he was not what I felt a brother should be. At bottom, the only thing we shared was that we happened to have been born to the same woman. I often wondered what my life would have been like if she had not been my mother, if I had been conceived in another womb or lived in another part of the world or if on the night I was conceived my father had been too exhausted to lift so much as a finger . . . I don't suppose it would have changed much. After all, there would have been countless other nights when he would not have been too tired to switch off the light and deposit me in her uterus. And then my mother would have said, "Aren't you done yet?" and nine months later out I'd have popped, or some other me with the same name, who would have lived like me and had the same thoughts I'm having now, like, "What if that evening . . . ?"

In order to set about my grand project of being a man, I embarked on minute observations of that alien species, especially my cousin Angelo. He was thirteen, with pitch-black hair and eyes and a perennial suntan from working outdoors helping Uncle Giovanni, whose nickname was "Hairy" and who was living proof of Darwin's theories. Angelo was solid, with lascivious eyes and nimble hands, everyone's stock image of a Sicilian teenager. He did not go to school because he didn't need to. He was clever, lively, and masculine without macho posturing.

17

I used to follow him around the countryside like a lost lamb. I would stand over him when he milked the scrawny, muddy goats and watch while he sucked a raw, new-laid egg with one gulp or when he shut himself away in the stable to smoke the cigarette butts discarded by his father. I would be close on his heels when he deliberately walked through the horse droppings because he thought it brought good luck and when he looked in the mirror to check the progress of his stubble. I copied everything he did, so, while my peers were lining up to paint their faces, I was locked in the bathroom, learning how to shave. I would lather my face expertly, then take the razor and very slowly (not for fear of nicking myself but because it seemed more stylish) remove the layer of foam from my cheeks. While the other girls were using up mountains of Kleenex and wiggling their hips, I spent much of my time scratching a gravely underendowed crotch. And while they maintained decorous composure even when sitting on the toilet, I surreptitiously practiced peeing standing up and spitting out of windows. My classmates made it a point of honor to swoon at the sight of a spider while I was enthusiastically capturing and dissecting them.

I made several attempts at chewing tobacco and soon, after a few initial difficulties, was managing to smoke up to thirty cigarette butts a day; I learned how to inhale and exhale nonchalantly through my nose. By this time, I was trailing Angelo like a shadow. I

18

didn't let him out of my sight and spied on all his activities. He only had to turn around and presto, there I was. Though he objected at first ("This is man's work, Annetta"), he was won over in the end. He was the only person I confided my secret to, not, you'll understand, voluntarily, but because once he peeped through the keyhole and caught me peeing standing up. There was no possible explanation without a full confession. Predictably, he greeted my announcement with gales of mirth, but when he saw I was completely serious, he appointed himself as my instructor.

From then on, he took me with him everywhere, even to the bathroom, where, standing shoulder to shoulder, we peed together. He taught me how to lob stones at tin cans, first with my eyes open, then blind-folded. He showed me how to spit through clenched teeth, head tipped back so the spittle would fall in an elegant curve, and how to dissect frogs and set mouse-traps. He taught me how to fool the guard dogs when we were stealing plump tomatoes from Uncle Vincenzo's orchard, how to strut like a boy and shake hands like a man. Then he showed me his father's dirty comic books. This was a complete eye-opener: during my religious phase I hadn't even been able to look at the illustrations of naked men in my science book. Too horrified even to touch the page, I would cover it with an exercise book or another of my text books. The comic Angelo had selected for me was *Snow White and the Seven Dwarfs*. I was rather taken aback by the fact that it seemed to have very little to do with the fairy tale. By page 5 I was flabbergasted: there was Snow White on all fours with her dress hitched up over her bare bottom and the kindly huntsman with his trousers around his knees and something very odd sticking out between his legs. Involuntarily, I found myself gazing at Angelo's crotch, then raised my eyes to his face. He was reveling in my discomfiture.

"Don't tell me you didn't know what men look like down there," he smirked. Well, okay, I had observed the way boys seemed to scratch between their legs all the time and naturally I had wondered why. Moreover, it hadn't escaped my notice that Angelo always turned his back on me when we peed together, so all I ever saw was his shoulder or, at the very most, a glimpse of bare bottom.

My apprenticeship had lasted barely two months, but it had been a time of hopes and dreams. Now I saw that it had all been pointless, that I would never be able to have that "thing," that without it I could never become a man, and that never, ever, would I be able to wear trousers.

So it was back to the old life of being a girl. I distanced myself from Angelo and spent all day moping around in my dull, long, navy pleated skirt.

At home, my bid for freedom had been forgotten and life had returned to normal. That is, my mother continued to hurl shoes at me for not helping with the housework, my father ditto because I had ruined his white shirt, and my brother because I had wrecked his razor.

Then Antonio left to look for work in Germany, and the house became more peaceful. Not that he was all that much of a nuisance, but it was a relief to have him out of the way. As it turned out, he stayed for seven years, met a girl whom he married, and had three children, one after the other. My parents had hoped he would give them some financial support, but there wasn't a peep out of him for the first four months and then it was only to ask *them* for money. From then on, he wrote asking for money every two to three months, complaining that he and his family were short of cash and that he must have at least enough to keep them all fed. When he married, he hadn't let us know for two months; he'd left it so late for the sake of the kids, he said. Finally, after seven years, he came home, with the excuse that he wanted to introduce us to his family, but there is no getting away from the fact that he is still unemployed and still living with my parents.

Antonio's homecoming was like something out of an American film. He blasted his horn for ages outside the house, and when I leaned out of the window, all I could see below was the front of what looked like an aircraft carrier with an elbow sticking out of the car window. He showered us with every kind of sweet under the sun; my favorites were the chewy ones that tasted of Coca-Cola. My mother was all over him the moment he walked through the door. She kept looking at him and couldn't stop smothering him with hugs and kisses. In all the excitement, it was some time before she registered the presence of four other figures standing behind him with bulging suitcases. They were all fair-haired, and looked skinny and exhausted. He introduced us to Karina his wife ("*Carina* Karina," said my mother) and the children, Giuseppe, Peter, and Ingrid. Naturally, they had barely a word of Italian between them except for the odd phrase like "You're a pain in the butt" or "Put a lid on it."

My mother rushed around like a maniac, piling their plates with almond tarts and spicy fruitcake while asking Antonio endless questions about life in Germany. From the way he told it, and their trendy clothes and the huge car parked outside, you'd have thought we were entertaining a millionaire, or nearly, in our midst. In the days and weeks that followed, he regaled us with stories about the large factory he owned and his high standing in the community. He told us all about the furniture and toys in his house in Cologne but somehow never seemed to have any plans for returning. In fact, by now he and his family were firmly installed in the house and my parents were having to support us all.

Later, of course, we learned that he had just been on the production line at the factory, that the famous modern house was rented, and his high standing in the community a figment of his imagination. What's more, the car was third- or fourthhand, and he had had to sell everything and pilfer from the factory in order to pay for it and the trip home. When they had caught him at it, all he could say was, "What's it to them, they've got plenty to spare." He was fired on the spot, packed up everything, and came home.

During those seven years I had been like an only child. I still went to school regularly, I still failed to shine, and I still merited no attention from my peers. They had forgotten about my religious aspirations, fully occupied as they were with perfecting their vampish images. Nothing had changed. They still wiggled their hips while crude comments and the headmaster's beatings proliferated. And, even though I was no longer surrounded by the odor of sanctity, I was still an outsider. All the same, school was the only area of interest and stimulation in my life. Otherwise, it got more and more meaningless.

I had reached that awkward age between adolescence and womanhood. Gone were the happy childhood days of playing in the yard with my friends or making scooters from dismembered fences and ball bearings filched from workmen. There was one scooter I especially loved, having managed to put it together and paint it bright yellow all by myself. We would hold races down steep slopes and sometimes even got as far as the sea.

We·were incredibly ingenious in finding ways of overcoming our lack of pocket money. If the mood took us, we would set ourselves up as street vendors, arranging a row of chairs in the piazza all laid out with clothes, tablecloths, and napkins that we had pinched from home. I can't say we had much success. In fact only one person ever showed any interest, a woman who came over to the stand because one of the table-cloths had caught her eye. The matter went no further — she noticed all the stains and tears and we never saw her again. There were all sorts of other ruses. We would go from door to door with collection plates and holy pictures to gather donations for the church. This venture was a bit more successful; we did scrape a few pennies together and decided to capital-ize by holding real masses in the courtyard behind my house.

These religious and criminal activities ran con-currently — the sacred and profane hand in hand, you could say. The escapades I remember most vividly are those in which my cousin Rosa and I were accomplices. We were nearly the same age and height and our mothers dressed us identically. People often mistook us for twins, though I couldn't see the resemblance myself. We were pictures of innocence when we set out in the mornings in our spotless little dresses and neatly braided hair. And how could we not avail ourselves of the limitless opportunities for delinquency afforded by our angelic appearance? We would steal big boxes of chocolates or candied fruit from under the noses of the shopkeepers without the least shame or remorse. While one of us distracted the shopkeeper, the other copped the goods. Then we would stroll nonchalantly out of the shop, get as far as the corner, and break into a run toward Villetta to gloat over our day's work. Chocolate and candied fruit have never tasted so sweet since.

As I said, I could no longer go about with my peers and playmates because we had lost the innocence of childhood. Now every gesture seemed to have malice behind it, every phrase could be misconstrued, and skinny-dipping was a thing of the past.

I nearly died of embarrassment when I started my periods. In this part of Sicily it is usual, or at least tradition dictates, that all the family should be in on this landmark in a girl's life, something which strikes me as offensive if not downright tasteless. My friends and I had gossiped and snickered about what lay in store for us, about becoming "a woman," developing breasts, and using sanitary napkins. Then one day, as I was sitting on the toilet, I saw the water turning red. I quickly shouted for my mother to tell her what had happened, reveling in the prospect of her embarrassed explanation. She kept her eyes down. "You know what this means, don't you?" I fixed her with a smile of beatific innocence. "No, Mom." "Oh, yes you do, my girl." And with that she flounced out.

I don't remember exactly when it happened, but I'm almost sure it was late evening, because the next morning the house was swarming with people who looked as if they had come to a wake. If it hadn't been for the smirks and knowing looks, you would have thought there had been a family tragedy. But I soon understood that the attention was all centered on me, and, since I was clearly alive and kicking, it looked as if my mother had wasted no time in spreading the news. Fleetingly, I thought of her as like the town crier of times past who made his rounds shouting out the names of lost children in ringing tones, but my reverie was interrupted by a flurry of eager hands, beaming smiles, and hugs that winded me. They congratulated me and wished me well while I blushed scarlet and managed to stammer out my thanks. Of course, men being men, my father was the only one not to mention it. In fact he steered well clear of the subject, not out of any regard for my feelings, I hasten to add, but purely because this was decidedly not men's talk.

In fact, I didn't feel any different and I was still virtually flat chested, so the various bras given me by my aunts, according to custom, were packed away in a chest along with my trousseau, which had been all prepared since I was five. All that was new, relatively speaking, was that I was once more seized with the desire to wear trousers. I asked Mother if I could, and her unwitting reply, "Good girls don't wear trousers. They're for men, or sluts," gave me my next idea. Easy, I thought: if I couldn't be a man, then I'd become a slut.

Before I go any further, let me tell you the local definition of a slut; it isn't a woman who sells her body to a rich, demanding man. Here, a slut is any woman who doesn't dress or behave in the way that is considered proper. Not that women like this are, by definition, promiscuous — in fact they hardly ever have a chance. "Slut" is just a convenient label, a license for gossip, and you could even say these women fulfill an important social function.

To understand that last phrase, you need some idea of how the villagers' minds work. It's not that anyone around here is really nasty — their passion for gossip isn't, as you might think, deliberately spiteful. It's just that the village has precious little to offer by way of recreation or fun of any kind, and the inertia

27

brought on by the heat makes for fertile imaginations. Gossip requires ingenuity and inventiveness to furnish all the required nuances, as detailed and colorful as a mosaic. It's much more than a simple statement of facts, it's a way of exercising the mind, a feast of fantasy. Okay, so it may not be the most savory activity, but people have to make do with what they've got. Hence the social value: our slut offers them a different point of view. You'd think they'd be grateful, but not a bit of it. Far from being appreciated, these social benefactors are slandered and treated like dirt. It's not as if this reaction is motivated by real malice — it's that the villagers' fevered minds are offended by the ordinariness of real facts, which make them feel fettered and degraded. So they nourish themselves with speculation on the pretty young things on their way to school or mass, determined to find something sinister in the way they walk, talk, or even genuflect. Of course, if they can't detect anything, it's time for the wilder flights of fancy. "I didn't see Rosetta at mass on Sunday," someone would say, sotto voce. "Yes, I wonder what she was up to, and with whom?"

All things considered, I could never have been the model daughter who only tags along with her parents to large parties in the hope of finding a husband. I was not the type to go along with my eyes cast demurely down, pretending not to notice if anyone looked at me, or to kneel at the altar on Sunday, looking all pious amid the murmur of old spinsters repeating their litanies year after year, counting every bead of their rosaries as if they were saying the Stations of the Cross. So what if I was declared a slut and my name bandied about? It would have been worth it to be able to wear trousers.

Through close observation, I had picked up many tips from my classmates on the techniques of seduction. I held back from buying lipstick, eyeshadow, and that kind of thing: I could not afford them, and I certainly could not ask my parents for money, so to begin with, I contented myself with watching the others from my usual corner. But soon I started edging my way toward them, eavesdropping on their world and tentatively asking my first questions. They treated me like a half-wit because my questions were so half-witted, but nothing would deter me. Little by little I succeeded in perfecting my hip-wiggling, and I hitched up my skirt just a fraction and rolled up lengths of toilet paper to pad out my flat chest. My attempts were decidedly awkward and earned me derision from the girls and snide remarks from the boys. However, one day, when I was in the cloakroom during recess, lady luck came to me in the shape of Angelina Carasotti, the engineer's daughter.

Angelina was a notorious "slut" who had only

recently come back to the village. She and her family had lived in northern Italy for thirteen years and she had been brought up quite differently from us Sicilians. She was allowed a freedom I envied and gave lots of parties to which very few of us were allowed to go but which were reported to be very lavish affairs with plenty of loud music. She was allowed to go out whenever she wanted and was never seen without an escort; there were always a handful of boys at her beck and call. What's more, she wore skintight trousers or flouncy organza skirts that blew up and showed her legs at the slightest gust. She was always laughing, showing off her gleaming mouth. Angelina looked everyone straight in the eye — she never lowered her gaze even when she was being told off by a teacher. She was very nearly expelled once because the math teacher ordered her not to look him in the eye in that way and she retorted, "I'll look where I please and if it bothers you, I suggest you look the other way."

Personally, I thought she was a show-off and a bit thick, but the others thought the world of her. Anyway, I suppose she must have felt sorry for me because I looked like such an idiot, however hard I tried. So, that day she came up while I was standing in front of the mirror the girls had put up, and she picked up a lock of my hair with "I think you'd look better with your hair up, don't you?" I gazed back at her in the mirror, speechless — all I could do was nod. Then she took me by the hand and led me into one of the bathrooms.

"You and I must have a talk." She sat on the toilet, flinging one leg over the other, and lit up a cigarette, inhaling deeply so that her mouth became a quivering glossy red heart. She fluttered her eyelashes, held her other hand motionless in midair, flat, as if she were holding a lampshade, then looked me in the eye and said, "It's not difficult to get the hang of, you know. You just need to work on it; I'll show you if you like." I stared down at her with awe and admiration, convinced that I could never hope to be as cool as she was, but determined to try as hard as I could.

From that day on, Angelina and I were virtually inseparable. She treated me as if she were setting about training a savage, and I was willing to undergo any humiliation. She was the first to show me how to apply makeup, experimenting with various powders to see which suited my coloring and choosing the eyeshadow most flattering to my eyes. She almost never lost her temper, however much I blinked when she was doing my eyes, or fidgeted or licked off the strawberry-flavored lip gloss. On the rare occasions when she did get angry, she still managed to maintain her composure. In all that time I never once heard her raise her voice, swear, or get rattled. The worst thing I remember her saying was, "Stand still, you moron."

She was always kind and attentive and never let a single detail escape her. She lent me her heels and set about teaching me how to walk in them. It was agony because my feet were a size larger than hers. I teetered along, supporting myself against the wall as if I had one leg shorter than the other. She was the one to rearrange the padding in my bra with tissues she'd plundered from her dowry trunk, and it was she who instructed me how to behave with boys.

"Now remember, boys always look there first. Faces come later."

She even taught me how to breathe properly. I had never realized how difficult it could be. Then it was how to speak, how to look and listen, how to act distant, how to laugh and smile seductively, how to look serious, how to eat, drink, sit, stand, how to pin up my hair and shake it loose sexily. She was a mine of trivial but invaluable information, and she dispensed it liberally.

"When you're talking to a boy," she confided one day, "you should always look him in the eye. Then when you're listening, look at his mouth, keeping your own lips slightly apart." "When you're attracted to someone, don't let on; you can flatter and flirt to begin with, but then pretend you don't care." She was a walking handbook of sexual know-how, and she always

knew the answers since everything about her was re-
hearsed and calculated.

Of course I followed her instructions to the letter,
never daring to add any ideas of my own. I turned into
her twin, which seemed to work wonders with the
boys. They were soon flocking around me with their
crude remarks. Angelina treated me as a protégée,
taking me with her wherever she went, and even invit-
ing me to her notorious parties. She wasn't actually
very fond of me though — indeed it was the last thing
I wanted — but I couldn't deny that she had me spell-
bound in the way that a child sometimes is with a
grownup. I idolized her. She always had a solution to
everything, and she lived the kind of life I longed for.
Still, in the end I wasn't really envious, because I never
once saw her laugh. What I mean is, I never saw her
laugh spontaneously, and I can't believe that someone
who isn't able to laugh is happy. She might have
thought she was having fun but she was never truly
happy. I could tell because her eyes were oddly dead,
and no amount of compliments could light them up.

Everyone assumed that Angelina's parties were virtually orgies, since, while there were always plenty of
boys strutting about like turkey-cocks, very few girls
were allowed to go. They were out of the question for
me: I could never have asked my parents' permission

because I knew what they thought about parties in general and Angelina's in particular. All I could do was dream about my initiation into that sleazy, thrilling world and try to invent some excuse to allow me to go to just one of them. Of course not one of my dresses was remotely trendy enough, but Angelina promised to lend me something. I racked my brains to think of some way to escape my house arrest and fulfill my dream for a few hours. Knotted sheets were out of the question; my absence would be noticed at once. Something much more subtle was needed.

Then Angelina had a brainstorm. The plan was for her to come to my house one afternoon and ask my father if I could go over to her house to study since I didn't have an encyclopedia at home. It was a terrific idea, except that I couldn't bear the idea of her seeing my home or meeting my parents. I had seen hers at school once; they were fantastically smart, and everyone talked about their beautiful house with its huge living room hung with oil paintings and a crystal chandelier. Then I thought of my mother with her bun and her hand-me-down clothes and my father slouching around with his muddy shirt hanging out. As for the house! I hardly dared think what she'd make of that. The one and only bedroom was sparsely furnished; there was an untidy bed in the middle of the room and a large cupboard and trunk. The kitchen had a table set against the wall, with four chairs, and we used the sink for washing the dirty clothes as well as the dishes. Smoke from the oven had blackened all the walls, and there was a minuscule bathroom that had a curtain instead of a door because my father had kicked it down when he locked himself in once. The toilet was open to the winds since it lacked a seat, and there was a large plastic tub that we used as a bath and the tiny storage room where I had my cot. Thank God my brother was still in Germany; otherwise we would all have had to share that cramped space as we had in the past.

I was ashamed of my family, of my home, and of who I was, and I was afraid of forfeiting Angelina's friendship once she saw how I lived. But how could I explain all this to her? I squirmed at the thought of her pure white dress against the background of our smoke-stained walls. My mother always insisted on baking her own bread in the oven, because she said you never knew what those bakers put in their bread nowadays.

When I broke the news that Angelina was coming that afternoon, she made the most almighty fuss about "people like that" sullying the home. I spun a yarn about Angelina and me being specially paired off at school, so there was no more to be said because the teachers knew best. So then Mom spent the whole afternoon cleaning the house till it shone. She even got down on her hands and knees and waxed the floors until you could almost see yourself in the tiles. The house looked immaculate, but the walls were still black and Angelina did indeed turn up in a white lace-trimmed dress. By this time my mother was a wreck, tired and sweaty, with her petticoat showing beneath her black dress, but Angelina seemed not to notice. Although Mom had cleaned and dusted the chairs, I still thought they weren't nearly clean enough for that immaculate dress and couldn't bring myself to ask Angelina to sit on them.

My mother, in an attempt at hospitality, offered her hot bread, its crust blackened by the oven, which only made matters worse. I squirmed at Angelina's embarrassment, wishing I could melt into those black walls, never to be seen again. Even the conversation was agony, because my mother spoke in Sicilian and Angelina replied in Italian while I just sat there dumb. I hated my mother at that moment, and knowing it wasn't her fault just made me hate her more.

Then my father turned up and inspected Angelina from the safety of the doorway, clearly amazed by what he saw. He gave her a grubby handshake, leaving smears on her white hand. As I saw her flinch, I hated my father too. But Angelina managed to stay all gracious and smiling, looking down bashfully whenever she spoke, so that my father was won over and gave me permission to study at her house the following evening, though only until seven because in his book it was dangerous for a girl to be out any later. Angelina persuaded him to extend the curfew to eight, promising that her parents would drive me home. Now all I could think about was next day's party, and I pushed those sooty black walls to the back of my mind to lose myself in the rose-tinted, stereotyped emotion of sentimental teenage comics and best-selling romances.

Why is it that at certain times of your life your thoughts are so banal and commonplace when you're sure they're utterly unique? Though perhaps it is not just that time but a whole life of recurring banalities, of illusory uniqueness. I felt that I was alone in dreaming of that party, those boys, and the dress I'd wear. I imagined making a striking entrance into a glowing room whose white walls were covered with paintings and, as people parted to make way for me, attracting gasps of admiration and a buzz of flattering comments that I felt I couldn't live without. What should have been just superficial change had now turned into a major psychological upheaval. I craved attention; I needed to have all eyes on me and to have the satisfaction of juggling all the invitations to dance. I was high on compliments, a compliment-aholic.

Of course I hardly slept at all, and a rest snatched

at recess didn't do anything for the dark circles under my eyes. At last the day of the party had come!

Angelina collected me at five. She listened attentively to my mother's final instructions about when I must be back, and then we made a run for it. I was still ashamed of our poverty, and this was made worse when we got to Angelina's house. It was not a palace or even a mansion, but to my eyes it was far more impressive than either. It had a front door in pale, shiny wood with a gleaming brass doorknocker, the corridor stretched as far as I could see, and there were rooms wherever I looked. Now that she was on her own territory, Angelina's behavior toward me changed dramatically. She scolded me for touching things, told me how common I was, said I was leaving footprints on the floor, fingerprints on the furniture, warned me not to touch this vase or that ornament. She made me feel utterly worthless. Then she led me to one of their two bathrooms — two between the three of them! The bathroom tiles were so shiny that you could see yourself in them, and they had a proper big bath, which didn't have a single scratch or rust stain. There were mats on the floor and a matching cover on the toilet seat, and there were two sets of immaculate towels. I scarcely dared to walk on those tiles in case my reflection disturbed the perfection of the surroundings.

I assumed that Angelina wanted to put on my makeup, so I asked her where I should sit.

"I hope you're not coming dressed like that," she said. "Have a bath first and use some of my perfume." I was mortally offended. Granted, I was poor, miserable, and half-starved, but one thing I wasn't was dirty. God knows I had spent at least an hour scrubbing myself in our tiny bathtub, I had checked my appearance in the mirror over and over again and had used so much talcum powder that the smell was making me sick, but dirty I wasn't. I kept quiet and Angelina departed after commanding me not to drip on the floor, to use the red towel, not the white one, which reminded me of the white dress she had worn to my house and of our sooty kitchen walls. I was ready to weep with rage and mortification, but she returned unexpectedly. I hurriedly pulled up my skirt.

"What do you think you're doing?" she said. "Why haven't you locked the door? I know you want to be a slut, but I'll thank you not to practice in this house."

"Sorry, I didn't mean . . ." I stammered.

She shut the door again, and I locked it behind her. How could I explain that not only did we have no key to lock our bathroom door, we didn't have a door at all because of Dad smashing it down, and that my mother was quite capable of barging in through the curtain while I was stark naked in the tub.

Anyway, the bath was full now. I tested it with my finger and climbed in. It soon made me forget Angelina and the curtain and our plastic tub, but a quarter of an hour later Angelina was outside, shouting at me, so I got out. I had spread my clothes on the floor so as to make sure that there would be no splashes on the tiles. Now I dried myself with the red towel, so timidly that I stayed damp all over. Next, in a fit of madness, I started spraying Angelina's perfume all over before gathering up my wretched clothes and opening the door.

"Now what have you done?" she asked, wincing with distaste as she had when my father shook her hand. "Had a swim in the perfume?" Then she glanced into the bath, saw the water and stared back at me. My immediate thought was that she had seen a bathful of gray water, that I really was dirty.

"Why haven't you let the water out?" she demanded. "There is such a thing as a plug, you know."

Perhaps I should have told her that water was so scarce at home that we only had baths every other week, that Mom had her bath after me and then used the water to scrub the chipped terracotta tiles that we sometimes tripped over. I apologized again but Angelina ignored me with a shrug, and when I asked if I could borrow one of her dresses, she said she'd better make me up first so that none of the green and blue eyeshadow got spilled on her dress.

✿ ✿ ✿

By half past six I was ready, my hair teased into a beehive, my eyelids painted turquoise, and my mouth scarlet. Angelina had lent me a blue organza dress and a pair of heels a size too small. The scooped neckline and full skirt that billowed out when I pirouetted made me feel like a princess. Then Angelina made her appearance, and I felt like a frog again. She was in a figure-hugging black dress, high at the front but split to the thigh and plunging almost to the waist at the back. Completing the picture, a cigarette dangled from those glossy, heart-shaped lips.

There was no striking entrance for me, no gasps of admiration, and the buzz of flattering comments was conspicuously absent. The only thing that corresponded to my fantasies was the glowing white room, which did indeed have paintings all over the walls. I had no idea whether they were worth anything; I just thought they were lovely. One in particular caught my fancy, with its ornate gold frame. Painted in rich, subdued colors, it showed a buxom blonde reclining naked on a bed. I thought it was perfectly beautiful and just stood there gazing.

Angelina caught sight of me in rapt contemplation and nudged me sharply.

"What's the matter with you?"

41

"I just think that's the most beautiful thing I've ever seen."

"Don't you know anything? It's complete crap."

Of course I knew nothing about art, as Angelina was well aware and as she pointed out derisively to her friends standing around. It made me start wondering what art was all about, why one picture could be labeled crap and another a masterpiece. Looking at that painting had filled me with the same indefinable feelings I got when I watched a sunset or gazed at the expanse of the sea. Were they crap? I supposed they didn't count as art, simply because they had always existed and always would. Their true value was that anyone could lay claim to them; they weren't the property of just one person. If looking at them gave you that feeling of love, they belonged to you. And because that picture had moved me so deeply, I had, in a way, made it mine. But Angelina would probably never feel anything deeply and because of that would never know the true value of anything, the secret joy of possession.

Predictably, there were hardly any female guests, three or four at most, but twenty or so boys, all bright eyed and bushy tailed. Needless to say, as the queen of local society, Angelina was the belle of the ball, laughing, flirting, now attentive, now bored, far too busy to look after the other girls languishing in the background.

The only person who showed the slightest interest in me was a boy called Nicola. He was about
twenty and very dark with striking blue eyes. I danced
with him all evening and told him a little about myself
while carefully avoiding the subject of my family. He
seemed very nice, and when he looked into my eyes I
forgot everything Angelina had taught me. Finally I
pulled myself together and remembered to stare at his
mouth with my lips half-parted, at which point he
started feeling me up. The courting ritual required a
show of outraged modesty, so I glared and pulled
away, and five minutes later of course he was at it
again.

And suddenly it was seven thirty and I had to go. I
found Angelina draped over a sofa being kissed by
some boy. I was beginning to worry because I hadn't
seen her parents all evening, so hesitantly I asked her
where they were. She said they were upstairs in the
bedroom and far too busy to take me home. I was in a
state of panic, but Angelina smirked and said that she
had already told Nicola to take me home. He smirked
back at her, all eagerness. I was terrified that my father
would see Nicola, but it was too far for me to get back
in time on foot, so I agreed. Anyway I was longing to
be alone with Nicola. I changed quickly and washed
off my makeup. Nicola gave me a hug and told me to
get into the car. During the drive he put his hand on
my knee and said all sorts of nice things.

"You've turned out to be quite a looker," was one of his compliments. I blushed scarlet but allowed his hand to stay where it was. When he dropped me off, he asked if he could see me the next day. What could I say? I wasn't even sure I'd still be alive by then. So of course I said yes, and he tried to kiss me, and I escaped into the house.

Naturally my father was waiting for me, standing on the balcony, his eyes fixed on the car. I was quaking as I went up the front steps and turned dizzy with relief when I realized he hadn't caught sight of Nicola. He had only seen the car and was now waiting to cow me with that look of his. As usual, he didn't subject me to questions; all the same he made me feel soiled and exposed. He just switched off the lights and sent me to bed.

At school next day, the girls eyed me with mingled hostility and admiration. When recess came, I was inundated with questions.

"So, how far did you go?" "Did he kiss you?" "Where did he touch you? Go on, tell us!"

It was my turn to be the center of attention, my turn to choose my answers carefully so as not to antagonize anyone, my turn to keep them guessing.

Then up came Angelina, announcing that Nicola had told her that we had a date. She too had a date that afternoon, with Enzo (who was not the boy she had been kissing on the sofa), and she suggested we make it a foursome, once more telling our parents we were studying together. Luckily my father bought our story again, and she and I went out at four thirty. There was no time to change at Angelina's because we'd arranged to meet the boys in Villetta at five. Angelina, though, said we mustn't be too punctual: keeping them waiting would "make us more desirable."

At last we all met up and sat down together on the park bench. Enzo's first move was to put his hand on Angelina's breast, so Nicola decided to try the same thing with me. Angelina didn't object, so neither did I. Then Enzo kissed her and she kissed him back, while Nicola and I followed their example. The only thing that mattered was that Nicola was a boy. It could have been Giuseppe, Giovanni, or Angelo for all I cared. I would have been equally happy in the arms of any one of them. No boy would ever cause me sleepless nights. My nights belonged to me exclusively, a precious time consecrated to my secret dreams that no mere boy would ever be allowed to intrude on. Nicola hadn't exactly swept me off my feet; it was just that I had to start somewhere. We didn't have anything to say to each other. Seated on that bench, he made the moves and I went along with them, utterly detached, his kiss simply a tongue pushing around inside my mouth.

While we were thus engaged an elderly man who

was walking past stopped, looked hard at us, then grabbed me and started hitting me on the face, yelling that I was a slut and a whore. It was my uncle Raffaele. He seized me by the arm and dragged me the whole way home. It hurt so much that I wasn't even able to think about what awaited me there. My father was still out working, but my mother was there, doing the ironing. My uncle told her, and to this day my arm has a great scar the exact shape of my mother's iron. I ran to lock myself in my room while she stood there, incandescent with rage. I didn't have long to wait for my father. He hammered at my door, ranting and cursing. I wouldn't unlock the door, so he broke it down. I remember thinking vaguely it was pity we didn't have curtains when the beating started and I passed out.

When I regained consciousness, I realized that my school days were over: my first pious ambition had been fulfilled and I was now a recluse. So had my more recent one, of becoming a slut, at any rate in my parents' eyes. Certainly, they treated me like one. From then on I was made to stay within the four sooty walls of the kitchen, gazing glumly at the loom and the jars of tomato sauce. It was evidently going to be some time before I could rehabilitate myself, before my transgressions would be forgotten so that my father could go in search of a man so uniquely high-minded that he could bring himself to overlook my murky past and marry me. That was the last thing I wanted, but sluts don't have any say in the matter, and no one was about to ask my opinion.

Every day brought new humiliations. Before long I was brought to such a pitch of desperation that I would have welcomed a husband, simply to escape my father's thunderous silences and my mother's lamentations. These conformed to a regular pattern. Her sobs would be almost inaudible sniffles to begin with but would gradually gather force until her weeping was a river, a torrent, a veritable ocean of tears. Over and over she moaned that never had she dreamed that a daughter of hers could ever . . . and then she'd dissolve again. Part of me began to feel that I really had committed the ultimate sin, but there was another part, the part that survives beyond time and space and brutality, which knew that I had done nothing wrong, at least toward my parents, and it was this that kept me from accepting their version of events. At the same time it took every ounce of willpower I had not to succumb to my mother's accusations. The worst of it was that she wasn't putting it on: it was agony for her that her only daughter, for whom she had had such high hopes, was the subject of gossip everywhere. Of course it wasn't "everywhere," though admittedly all the mothers were talking about it, and that was torture enough for her.

47

Uncle Raffaele had jumped at the chance of blackening the name of his detested brother. For a whole month my mother never ventured out of the house unless she absolutely had to, and when she did, she kept her eyes on the ground like all those other mothers of so-called sluts. But there was no letting-up: at any hour of day or night the house would be full of relations from both sides of the family, all eager to commiserate with her over the family disgrace. It might be Aunt Nunziatina with her pearls of proverbial wisdom ("You can't touch pitch without being defiled"), or Aunt Ntunina, who would stay for over an hour, crying the whole time, or Aunt Milina grumbling about the youth of today and lamenting "the good old days" when everyone had arranged marriages. Then there was Aunt Ciccina, who brought my mother baskets of food as though she were convalescing from a dreadful illness, averring that there was nothing in the world worse than hunger.

Only Uncle Toto and Aunt Mimmina were conspicuously absent, finding reasons to be out of the neighborhood; the whole affair was a painful reminder of their sixteen-year-old daughter Cettina, who some months before had eloped with the son of Mastru Giovanni, the bricklayer, and hadn't been heard of since. They refused to inform the police because they "didn't want the whole world talking about it," even though they knew perfectly well that there wasn't a soul who didn't seize on it as a subject for gossip. My mother, though, was very glad to be spared their presence. She could not have borne the fact that they were in the same boat; she just wanted to be left alone. From the way she was acting it was clear that for her a problem shared was *not* a problem halved. She was going through torments and couldn't bear being encouraged to "have a good cry" or, even worse, being told to cheer up. She didn't want to cheer up, she just wanted to be left alone with her grief. So during these visitations she would assume a fine indifference, acting as if she had never had a daughter and just mumbling, more to herself than to anyone else, "My daughter died a month ago . . . I don't have a daughter anymore." At which, she'd burst into fresh tears and have to suffer the humiliation of the visitors' encouraging words and stock phrases of consolation. She would thank them all for coming, knowing perfectly well that the moment they left they would be reveling in her discomfiture, just as she had reveled in that of Uncle Toto.

I vividly remember her coming home that time, a smug smile on her face and full of patronizing remarks and complacent sarcasm at his expense. So it was hardly surprising that she suffered such torments from the smirks of satisfaction, the pleasure in the fact that the tables had been turned. How could she bear the knowledge that under all the apparent sympathy lay a gleeful malice, and, above all, how could she bear not hearing a single word of remorse or explanation from her "fallen" daughter, who still had the nerve to eat, drink, crap, and pee, who still had the audacity to live and breathe? How on earth, I asked myself, did she put up with this charade? In fact, the truth was that she couldn't.

Soon her lamentations, which had never exactly been remarkable for their restraint, became ever more hysterical. She would utter the most tremendous sighs and moans, then collapse in a heap before getting up again. This process was repeated all day and every day, and she had even given up preparing meals, which meant that now my father's bitter complaints were added to hers.

I watched these goings-on from behind my door, or rather, from the curtain cut out of an old sheet that had been put up after Dad broke it down that day of doom and ventured out only to go to the bathroom. So I saw her dramatic collapses from a merciful distance, a blessing in disguise in some way, though it probably made me take her falls more seriously than they deserved. But I started having visions of cracked skulls, brain hemorrhages, and other such horrors. On one occasion I was really frightened: usually she'd pick herself up after a moment or two and start moaning again, but this time her collapse was followed by the sound of a plate breaking and then by absolute silence. In any other family, it would have been assumed that the plate had been hurled to the ground in a fit of impotent rage. But I had been a member of this family for over fifteen years, and I knew something was wrong. She always kicked up the most appalling fuss if my brother or I had the bad luck to drop a glass. In our house, a broken plate was considered a major disaster, and my mother kept a tally of every single one. Never in her wildest moments would she have dreamed of breaking a plate on purpose. This was worry enough, but more worrying still was that this time my mother lay there without moving. I gave her ten seconds, then twenty . . . thirty . . . but lost count in my anxiety and started thinking the worst.

I had a vision of her lying there in a pool of blood while I bent over her trying to revive her, and my father or one of my uncles suddenly appearing (because naturally, if unluckily, the door was ajar) and finding me with her lifeless body, blood all over my hands and dress . . . I would be arrested for matricide, and before you could say knife, and in spite of lengthy legal delays, there I'd be, condemned for life to a cramped dirty cell, surrounded by dyed-in-the-wool criminals, and it wouldn't do me the slightest bit of good to protest my innocence because nobody would believe me and not a soul would come to visit me. All these thoughts passed through my mind in those first seconds . . . to be followed by another scenario, gleaned from a mystery novel.

This time I was the victim, not the murderer. My mother had pretended to fall and had deliberately broken a plate so as to lure me from my room. Having caught me off guard, she would be able to carry out a merciless killing and make it look as if the breakage was an accident. . . . However, it soon occurred to me that she had probably never seen a crime movie in her life, never picked up a single Agatha Christie novel, and that her only outlet for creative fantasy was gossip. The worry about what had happened was conjuring up increasingly lurid and gloomy fantasies, so I made up my mind to venture out and have a look.

What I beheld was pretty lurid and lent substance to both my scenarios. There lay my mother beside the kitchen table, her outflung hand just touching one of the pieces of broken plate. That was the first scenario, but as I got close, her hand closed convulsively on the sharp fragment and I thought my last hour had come, forgetting that I had already seen the inherent implausibility of my second scenario. She started struggling to rise, and I stepped back instinctively. She dragged herself up by the table, and, after a stab of terror as she turned toward me, I felt profound relief: she looked so surprised to see me that I knew she couldn't be a murderous robot, programmed to kill me. But the sight of me must have reminded her of Uncle Raffaele dragging me in by the arm, announcing that he'd caught me in Villetta making a slut of myself with some boy. She instantly recovered from her short-lived fit and lunged toward me, her eyes darting around for something to hit me with. While I scurried from corner to corner, trying to find shelter from her fury, she hurled such bitter imprecations that I would far rather have been showered with the more customary shoes or plates or vases. Every word she spoke, or rather yelled, rattled out like machine-gun bullets, as if she was afraid of skipping a single phrase of the abuse crowding her brain. "Rot in hell," she cried, and "May your corpse be scraped off the street," or "Die, like the Jezebel you are," along with such felicities as "Scum," "Trollop," "Whore," "Prostitute."

And all the time, she was chasing me around the kitchen. She could never keep still when she yelled at me — indeed the shouting seemed to give her more energy. In fact, because she couldn't do what she really wanted, which was to hang me out of the window and beat me like a carpet, she got angrier and angrier until she collapsed in a heap on her bed. I wasn't so rash as to think that she had tired herself out. She was indefatigable, as I knew only too well from the times I'd gone shopping with her. What I think happened was that she had run out of insults. I had already observed that in her last bout she told me to rot in hell several times. Having spent most of my childhood squabbling with cousins of both sexes, I knew how humiliating it was having to resort to the same abuse you'd used a few minutes earlier, particularly if there were people watching. They're disappointed in their high hopes, and you end up with your mind a total blank, praying for inspiration so as not to lose face, and completely forgetting what the quarrel was about. And when at last you do come up with something, not only do you feel a sense of triumph, of pride in the richness of your vocabulary, your powers of invention, it also reflects well on your friends, to know such a mistress of invective, and even your opponent is proud to engage such a worthy opponent.

I knew very well how my mother's mind worked, though I realized that this wasn't the time to tell her so. It wouldn't have been safe; I needed to show her I was on her side. So I beat a retreat to my lair.

However, I was not (as I'd hoped) to number this incident among my many attempts to flee my home and my mother's wrath. In fact, it was to herald a new stage in my life. From then on she kept to her bed, moaning that she never wanted to see me again, that I'd taken ten years off her life, no, twenty years, thirty, that I was a dog returning to its vomit and would be better off dead and so on, before dissolving into noisy sobs again. So when my father got back to find her in this state, they decided it was time for me to leave. It should be clear by now that he didn't arrive at this drastic decision through any concern for my mother, still less because my presence had become an affront to him. After all, he had always succeeded in treating me as if I didn't exist. No, the reason he put his foot down was that Mom hadn't made him a hot meal for over a week. She hadn't cleaned the house either, and he had had enough of coming home from a hard day's work and having not only to prepare his own meal but also to attempt force-feeding her. It made no difference to me whether she cooked or not because I ate out of cans anyway, or crept out at night to steal ham or salami and bits of leftover cheese.

All right! I was to be sent away. The next problem was where to send me so that I would be safely out of sight and they wouldn't have to hear anything about me. As usual, I eavesdropped on the whole conversation, hanging on their every word and thinking about where I'd like to go, delighted at the prospect of escaping my mother's tears and tantrums.

Hope springs eternal, and I prayed that they'd send me to Aunt Camilla in Rome. It seemed the perfect solution: a long way from home, quite far enough to spare them the knowledge that people were gossiping about me, if that's what they wanted. But it was a nutty idea. My father thought Rome was a cesspool of decadence. God knows, I had heard him say so often enough to Aunt Camilla and her husband and children, who were allowed to "run wild." So where would it be? I was soon to find out. My mother still wasn't doing any housework or cooking, and my father wanted things settled as soon as possible.

One evening he got home, tired as usual and, as usual, asked my mother what there was for dinner. She told him that she had not got around to cooking because, as usual, she was feeling ill. As usual, he shouted and swore, then sat down and began to prepare something. When his meal was ready, he shouted at Mom to get out of bed and come and sit with him. He had something to tell her.

"Guess who I saw today? It was Vincenzino, and —"

"He knows all about it, doesn't he? Your own sister's husband, and he knows everything. . . . To think of the disgrace —"

"Shut up, will you, woman, and let me get a word in. Yes, he had heard . . . Oh, stop blubbering. I can't stand it any longer. Yes, of course he knows."

He turned aside and gnawed at a piece of bread. "Now look what you've done: you've made me lose my appetite." She dried her eyes, begging him to continue and promising not to cry.

"All right, if that's a promise, I'll go on. . . . Where was I? Oh yes, I saw Vincenzino, and he asked me if what he'd heard about Annetta was true. . . . Oh, come on, if you start again, I swear I won't say another word. Damn, now I've forgotten what I was saying."

I was on tenterhooks behind my curtain, dying to offer various helpful suggestions. But I hung on for what came next.

"Are you finished? Sure? Well, as I was saying, Vincenzino said they hadn't been around because Vannina was ill. I told him you were out of sorts too, and he asked why. Anyway, to cut a long story short, he said Annetta could stay with them. No problem, he said, honest. Vannina still doesn't feel too good and could do with some help around the house, and Annetta could live there as long as we wanted."

"So what did you say?"

"I told him he could keep her for good if he liked."

Up to now, I had been quiet as a mouse, hanging on their every word. But this was the last straw. I lost my head and shot out, screaming, "NO, NO, NO . . . I absolutely refuse to stay with Uncle Vincenzino. I won't, I won't!"

Mom lunged toward me, shouting, while my father tried to calm her. "Gently, gently. Let her have her say."

It was too late. I had clammed up with shame. My father persisted, ignoring my blushes.

"Speak up, then. What have you got against going there? Now listen here, my girl, we've had more than enough of your little ways. What I say goes, and I say you're to get out of this house tomorrow."

"I'll kill myself first. It's the last place I'd go to, and you know very well why."

"That's enough of your lip. You're a liar as well as being a little trollop."

I slunk off to my room to cry and brood over the experience of six years earlier that I had almost managed to forget.

It was when I was almost ten. At that time I used to spend more time with my grandmother than I did with my parents. We were a close family, and all the uncles and aunts on my father's side congregated at her house with their children. And I seemed to be the favorite child — indeed everyone called my grandmother "Annetta's Granny." I was spoiled rotten by my aunts and uncles, who gave more attention to me than to their own children.

It was a really happy time for me. I would go to my grandmother's house after school, often staying until dark. Sometimes I even slept there. I remember long peaceful afternoons playing with my friends and cousins. Sometimes we would go over to Aunt Vannina, who knew lots of ghost stories and some wonderful games. She was my father's youngest sister, lively and high-spirited, and still had something of the child about her. As children, we loved visiting her because it was so much more fun than in our own homes. When she played with us she was on our wavelength, but she also had a way of bringing us up to her level, of making us feel grown-up and responsible. She often made us help her with washing the steps, doing the dishes, or soaking the laundry without giving us anything in return, but we didn't mind because we loved and admired her so much. In fact we even volunteered to do these chores, which we would have avoided like the plague at home. Always patient and good-tempered, she knew intuitively how to treat us. I never saw her raise a hand to any of us. When she reprimanded us, she did so kindly and she seemed to love us all equally, so there was never any bickering or jostling for her attention. We were secure in the knowledge of her impartial love.

What was extraordinary was that she didn't even show favoritism toward her own children; she was everyone's Aunt Vannina. She lived in an old house near my granny and almost every afternoon the few rooms were swarming with a rabble of children carrying buckets, sponges, and cloths. I was always happy when I was there because she was such fun and so kind, but I loved my granny even more. Not that *she* was fair, to put it mildly. As I said, she loved me more than the others and made no attempt to conceal it, even when the other grandchildren were there with their parents. To be honest, I don't think I was conscious of it at the time, or if I was I certainly suppressed my consciousness. Needless to say, the others preferred the company of my aunt.

Aunt Vannina often invited me to stay the night and my parents never raised any objections. As I said, my aunt and grandmother lived almost next door, so my parents thought there was nothing to worry about. Later, my aunt moved to a district on the far side of the village, and it became much more difficult to spend some time with her, as my parents would only give permission on special occasions. I really missed those idyllic afternoons and I suppose my aunt must have missed me too, because one day she asked my parents if I could come and stay for a while. She succeeded in persuading my father, although he put up some objections to begin with, more from some vague notions of paternal duty than out of any real concern for me. Unexpectedly, it was my grandmother who kicked up a fuss. She was vehemently against the idea because she couldn't bear me to be away from her for more than half a day. It was only by exploiting her indulgent love that I was able to win her over, but in the end she threw up her hands and told me I could go.

My aunt's house was flanked by a pond and seemed to be in the real country, far from the crowded streets of the village. It was surrounded by woods and fields, and in the early morning the shepherds passed by with their flocks, and you could watch them doing the milking in the open air. I was thrilled by the

Don't Wear Trousers

invitation and felt especially privileged as the only one
out of all the nephews and nieces to have been chosen.

My aunt and uncle were complete opposites. She
was active and generous, while he was apathetic and
idle. I remember that when they still lived next door to
Granny, my aunt was always waiting up for him, often
until late. Once I had to help her cart him home from a
bar because he was too drunk to get back on his own.
Aunt Vannina worshiped her daughters and would
have done anything for them, however menial, to
make up for her husband's conspicuous lack of em-
ployment and initiative. They really were hard up: I
remember once my cousin asking the butcher if she
could have a ham roll on credit. He sent her away with
a reprimand, though he must have known that it
wasn't because of an idle craving but because she was
half-starved.

My aunt suffered appallingly under humiliations
like these because she longed for her children to have
the best of everything. At one time Uncle Vincenzo
went to work in Switzerland, but he came back less
than a year later with nothing to show for it except a
fling with a Swiss girl. To make ends meet for her
family, including her slob of a husband, my aunt did all
sorts of odd jobs — scrubbing staircases, giving injections, and baby-sitting demented old men.

When I arrived she met me with a wonderfully
warm welcome. She ushered my parents in and sat

61

them down to olives and cheese, sending me off to
play with my cousins. After half an hour my parents
came to say good-bye because they had to get back. As
it was getting late, my aunt told us to get into our
nighties while she prepared chicken broth. It was
winter, and her steaming hot dishes, redolent of the
country, did more for us than a hundred blankets. My
aunt, being who she was, kept us enthralled with every
mouthful by adding new details and incidents to her
never-ending Piddu and Puddu, Chidda and Nuddu
stories. Then she tucked us in bed, and we fell asleep
at once. I have never known a child suffer from insom-
nia, and I know I never did until the incident I'm
about to relate.

When I woke up next morning, I was the only
child left in the house — the others had gone to
school, but I had been allowed to stay home. It was a
real holiday for me. I went into the kitchen and saw
Aunt Vannina just about to go out. I asked where she
was going, and she said she was off to a neighbor's to
collect some vegetables. She told me I would be
quite safe, as my uncle was at home and he would
look after me. I stayed in the kitchen to eat breakfast.
As I was sitting there drinking my glass of fresh milk,
I sensed someone behind me, looked around, and
there was my uncle. I was always uncomfortable in
his presence, because he seemed bad tempered all
the time and hardly ever spoke to us children. He

looked at me in silence for a while, then said, "So does it taste good?"

I nodded and went on drinking my milk, still ill at ease. I don't remember all the details precisely, but he pulled a chair up close to me and sat down. Then he lifted my skirt and slid a finger into my vagina. I honestly don't remember what went through my mind as he did this. Probably Freud got it right about the way we suppress traumatic experiences, because my recall of the event is hazy and the words that come back to me reverberate in my mind as if amplified in an echo chamber until they become unintelligible.

Anyway, I've no idea how long he kept poking or whether he spoke to me at all. But one thing I am sure of and that is that I didn't tell him to stop or make any move to stop him. My aunt returned, and as Uncle Vincenzo stood up, he said solemnly, "We'll continue another time."

That evening my father arrived with my grandmother to fetch me home.

I didn't understand what he'd done to me then; I had not understood while it was happening, and I didn't for a long time afterward. This isn't as odd as it sounds. I know that I wasn't that young, but who was there to tell me that what he had done was wrong? My grandmother? Well, she was old and it wasn't her responsibility. My mother? Well, I've already told you how she dealt with, or rather shied away from, the subject of my periods.

The prospect of him coming back for more should have hung over me like the sword of Damocles, but I remained oblivious to it. In fact I didn't really think of it as a threat; because he hadn't blackmailed me or sworn me to secrecy I naturally assumed that it wasn't worth hiding. And if it wasn't worth hiding it couldn't be very bad. So I forgot all about it, or at least I thought I had, until a few months later when my cousin Rosa started telling me about her periods and lots of other curious things connected with sex. What she said brought back my strange experience, as the things she was talking about seemed to have some connection with what had happened. So, showing off a bit in the way one does when one doesn't want to be left out of anything, I artlessly told her what Uncle Vincenzo had done to me.

Perhaps it was just as well that I didn't keep my mouth shut, because I was at last made aware of the seriousness of what had happened. I say "perhaps," because Rosa's reaction took me completely by surprise. She was absolutely horrified. When she got her breath back she said it was the most disgusting thing she had ever heard.

Just then Granny was in the hospital, having been taken ill a few days earlier. Her gum-chewing young

64

doctor announced bluntly that it was a heart attack. I had no idea what this involved, but his impassive expression made me feel that there was nothing much to worry about. When Rosa made it clear that what my uncle had done was wicked, I was too scared to tell my mother. I thought she might beat me for lying. Most of all, I dreaded her reaction. If it seemed so appalling even to my favorite cousin, what on earth would my mother say? It had to be my grandmother, whose love and sympathy I had always been able to rely on. So, sitting on her bed, I told her.

"Annetta, are you sure you're telling the truth?"

I nodded. She burst into loud sobs.

"Oh my God, the filthy pig! Dirty child molester!"

Three days later she died. My mother had always been close to her so I wasn't surprised when, a few days after the funeral, she examined me in the presence of my brother.

"Is it true, that garbage you told your granny?"

Embarrassed, I could only nod.

"You silly bitch, why didn't you just shut up? It killed her, you know. Your granny's death is on your head."

And no one ever raised the matter again.

I still can't quite believe it. There were my mother and father in a state of permanent frenzy about my reputation and the family honor, and yet this didn't seem to trouble them one bit. I'm not talking about my own feelings; it's them I'm worried about. For me it was another matter altogether. For years I lived with the violation — not only what he did to me that time, but the violation of his visits to the house to be greeted warmly by my parents, the violation of sitting and listening to his small talk, of being asked why I didn't have a kiss for my old uncle after I'd kissed Aunt Vannina, when all I wanted to do was spit in his face. It was a violation having to keep my loathing and contempt to myself, and the final outrage was the burden of sin that I had persuaded myself I bore, the sin that he had committed and the sin of which I knew God accused me, since my mother had told me I was to blame for my grandmother's death.

I chose to banish that memory to stop myself thinking about that and my poor dead grandmother whose memory was the only beautiful, untainted thing I had left; I chose not to retrace that path, the path of my childhood. But in spite of this I am still a bad sleeper, haunted by nightmares, and always needing to keep a light on. At least once a week I dream that my uncles are taking turns to molest me. Only recently I dreamed that my brother and father were doing it too. The irony is that I never dream of *him*.

And now, in my disgrace, I was being sent back there, only too aware that there was unfinished business between us. His soft-spoken threat, "We'll continue another time," hung over me. I had always thought that my parents didn't believe me, but I couldn't see how they could be so harsh as to send me there for who knows how long. It was clear that they no longer regarded me as their flesh and blood, but surely this did not give them the right to jeopardize my self-respect.

I stayed awake all night trying to find a solution. I thought about escaping, informing the police, finding someone to protect me, killing myself . . . anything to avoid going to *him*, but my father had stationed himself outside my room to sabotage any attempt at fleeing his irreversible decision. I couldn't sleep. I heard the chimes of the clock hour after hour, feeling like the sacrificial lamb at the approach of Easter. I resented this feeling, since I had given up my fanciful ideas about monastic life and was no longer given to pious masochism. It was clear that their minds were made up, that my life was in their hands, and that there was nothing I could do. I saw my father silhouetted against the curtain as he sat there grimly with his arms folded. Around three thirty, I tried to speak to him, to explain my fears, but all he could say was:

"What are you afraid of? You want to be a slut, at least do it properly. Don't you want it, then? Oh yes, I nearly forgot, you prefer them young and handsome. Enjoy it and then have a good sleep, that's what I say."

I couldn't tell whether he was being serious or not. And I don't know which would have been worse: that he could joke, however savagely, over something so important, or, if he was serious, that he could even think of throwing me and my innocence, which was all I had to offer, to the wolves. Because that's what it amounted to. Nor, come to think of it, can I understand what my uncle did. I might have been able to understand — though never forgive — if I had been one of those luscious nymphets who seem to drive older men wild, who seem to bring out fantasies of possession, violation even. But I was such a scrap of a thing, the mother's milk scarcely dry on my lips as they say in these parts. I was virtually flat-chested at sixteen, so you can imagine what I looked like at ten, a walking, talking plain of Lombardy. There wasn't much of anything else either. I mean, what can you expect from a girl who hasn't even reached puberty? Oh, what's the use? It would take all the resources of psychiatry to fathom someone like Uncle Vincenzo.

All that time, I found myself returning to the incident again and again, with mingled revulsion and pity. Revulsion for him, for what he was, and pity for his daughters, who were nearly teenagers by now and who were undoubtedly at risk just being in the same house. After all, if he messed around with me, what was to stop him from doing the same with his daughters? I don't think he felt any guilt; he thought of what he was doing as normal. Otherwise, why didn't he swear me to secrecy? But my poor cousins had no one to protect them from their own father.

As all these thoughts were passing through my mind, I realized that twice that night I had looked on fathers as people to be fled from, and if you can't trust your own father, who can you trust?

Everything I had been taught as a child lay in ruins. All that stuff about not taking sweets from a stranger, or getting into cars with strange men, was so much nonsense. We should have been taught to watch out for the people closest to us: our parents, our relatives, and our friends. We know instinctively that we shouldn't trust strangers, and anyone silly enough to trust the first person who comes along has only himself or herself to blame. But who has ever warned us against you? Who should we blame if we die at your hands? Should we put it down to our blind faith in you?

I resolved that when I had children the first thing I'd teach them would be to guard against us, their parents, and I'd tell them so every day, every month, every year, until I had wiped out every trace of that silly confiding instinct that children have to trust any being who favors them with the odd kiss or hug, a being who is your parent only by chance. It could be anyone, and you could grow fond of them in the same way and put your life in their hands because, when it comes down to it, we are all like spaniels looking for a kind master, a master who might beat us if we stray but who, above all, protects us. But who will protect us from that master? Another master, from whom we'll need protection again, and so on, ad infinitum. We can never be safe until we understand that life is too precious to be placed arbitrarily into someone else's hands, rather than our own. When the time came I would teach my children to be themselves, to be their own masters and not to have to rely on anyone, not even us, their parents.

But, in spite of these thoughts, all I wanted was for my father to throw his arms around me and tell me he would never leave me. I longed for him to say that he'd stick by me and protect me from all the Uncle Vincenzos of this world. . . . I was feeling so helpless when I should have been trying to be powerful, invincible. . . . But there was no sign of my father coming in to hug me, so instead I hugged and mumbled at my pillow, reflecting that my grandmother wouldn't have allowed all this to happen. She would have held me tightly as she always did, winter or summer, when I slept in her bed. It was so funny, the way we slept together. We would lie there, our arms around each other, my strong little legs squeezed between her flabby old ones, while I rested my head on her kind, sagging breasts. I would be curled up like a fetus, and the strange thing was that, when I woke up, I would be in exactly the same position. Strange, because I was usually a restless sleeper. Now I think that she rearranged me in that position when she got up, much earlier than I did, but it was lovely to think I had stayed peacefully in that position all night. However it was, it's still lovely that that's what she wanted me to think. I always thought I would only marry a man who could hold me like that all night long. For the moment, though, I had to make do with my pillow, which, however, I always woke up to find on the floor or pushed to the end of my cot.

The thought of my grandmother, and that she might be looking down on me, was so comforting that I began talking to her as though she were in the room. "Granny, I'm sorry I haven't spoken to you all this time. . . . You know why. It's because Mom says you died because of what I told you. I don't believe her, but if it's true, I swear I didn't mean to. . . . I hope you'll forgive me too for not coming to see you when you were laid out, but you know that kind of thing frightens me and you wouldn't want me to be afraid of you, would you? I don't even know what they've done to your house because I haven't been there since you died. Listen, Gran, I want to ask you a favor. You know that your son wants to send me to *him*? Oh please, Granny, don't let them. He said he'd 'continue another

71

time,' and I don't know what to do. Dad has completely lost interest in me: you've seen what he does
and how he treats me. I know it was wrong to carry
on like that with a boy, but Granny, you don't think I
deserve this, surely. Come on, Gran. I'm only young.
If I don't make mistakes now, when can I? When I'm
so old and decrepit that I can't put one foot in front
of the other? And you must have seen how secretly
delighted all the relatives are with my disgrace. They
may pretend to care for me, but you were the only
one who really did. Oh, Granny, why did you die?
Why did you leave me all alone? I beg you, help me.
Explain my predicament to someone up there. It's
not important enough for God of course, but there
must be a saint or two who would be willing to listen.
Take him aside and tell him the whole story and say
I'll light lots of candles for him when they let me out
of here, and go to mass every Sunday and always put
something in the collection plate, and I won't yawn
once, even if I'm worn out. What do you think,
Granny? Will that do the trick? Because if not, I'll do
anything you think is necessary, okay?" And much
comforted, I fell asleep.

My parents called me only a few hours later. My father
shouted that it was past eight and high time I packed. I
leaped out of bed. It was a few minutes before I

recalled my prayers of the night, or the early morning to be precise, and I shot a silent, sarcastic thank-you at my grandmother and all those saints of hers up in heaven. I couldn't believe that out of three hundred thousand saints there wasn't one who wasn't too busy to help me out. Surely she could have found just one. Okay, I hadn't given her much time, but time can't matter all that much in eternity. I could see I was in for a long wait.

And then, just for a second, an image flashed into my mind. I tried to make it out but it became confused with details from what I had been dreaming just before I woke. It had seemed that my grandmother was with me, though I kept telling myself she was dead. She must have read my thoughts because she said that my dream was accurate . . . that she really had died and really was in heaven. I asked what life was like up there, and she said she was being very well looked after and had spaghetti with sauce every day. I can't remember what else she said, but it was strange that I'd dreamed of her now, when I hadn't had one dream about her since her death, not even the night she died. I like to think that she hadn't appeared earlier because she thought I wasn't yet ready and didn't want to upset me with her presence, that she had waited until I willed her, called on her. But try as I might I couldn't interpret that dream. The only thing I was sure of was that not even she had come to my rescue. I felt even more depressed, even more alone and unsure of my-self, even more desperate for love.

Meanwhile, the house was seething with prepa-rations for my departure. My mother bustled around looking for suitcases, cartons, bags, and baskets. She went at my drawers like a madwoman, throwing every-thing I possessed into the cases. Helping her for once, my father went through the house with a fine-tooth comb, not only searching for my belongings but weed-ing out every last object I might ever have come in contact with. They were bent on ridding the house of any trace or smell of me, the sooner the better. Mom commented on every article of clothing she was stuff-ing into the case; first it was my red skirt with black polka dots ("That stuff's not worth the money you squandered"), then it was my green woolen blouse ("Just look at that! It belonged to my sainted mother, and now that little trollop's tainted it"), and so on, grumbling about everything, my white shirt, my blue jacket . . . each item gave her a chance to moan about what I'd done, more excuses to get at me.

"Spare the rod and spoil the child, I say. Maybe if we'd beaten her more she wouldn't have turned into the slut she is."

Eventually the grand opera petered out and Mom burst into tears again. I hoped this new outburst might be a sign of belated remorse, timely and auspi-cious for me at least. I saw that a mother doesn't stop

74

being a mother, whatever happens, that however wicked I was I was her daughter, whether she liked it or not. I turned to her, frantic with despair.

"Oh, Mom, please, I beg you. Don't send me there."

My hopes couldn't have been more misplaced. If I hadn't been out of my mind with worry, I would have known how vain they were. Sure, Mom was in floods of tears, but she was weeping for herself, not for me. She was devastated at the thought that Aunt Vannina might spread the word about the disgrace I had brought on the family and kept on about not washing dirty linen in public, though even her precious proverbs didn't seem to do anything for her. So she started yelling at me again and, not content with this, began chasing me around the house. She took me by surprise and grabbed me by the hair, forcing me down till she was scrubbing at the floor with my ponytail twisted in her fingers. It was my father who finally stopped her by saying, "Oh, let her be, we're just wasting time."

This was the only argument that would have convinced her. She let go and my hair was given a breather.

My father was in high good humor, doubtless already looking forward to getting back home and having my mother, finally rid of my polluting presence, return to her housewifely duties. In his mind, I

knew he was already digging into that plate of suc-
culent spaghetti covered in tomato sauce made from
his mother's special recipe, so he hastened to pile my
things in Uncle Vittorio's delivery van and yelled at us
from the street to get a move on.

I noticed that my mother had a strange expression on her face. She was still railing at me and giving
me the occasional pinch, but her eyes were sad and
she seemed to be dawdling. Probably I was just imagining it out of a desire not to feel utterly rejected, but I
had the feeling that her final "Go to hell" had a touch
of melancholy: that her last pinch was a kind of caress,
her way of saying, "You'll always be my daughter, no
matter what." Doubtless I was mistaken or they
wouldn't have sent me there. My father was still shouting from the street, and Mom hastily closed the last
suitcase. I kept my head down, suffering all her abuse
and pinches and taunts. It was difficult not to fight
back, not to tell her exactly what I thought of her, but
I did not want to blow my chances in case there was
still a possibility, however remote, that they'd change
their minds. She thought I had come to my senses
and resigned myself to their actions — "So you've
climbed down, have you?" — but nothing could make
her relent.

At last we all got into the delivery van and Dad
started up the engine. I was next to the window, feeling like a chained prisoner being carried off to prison.

Anyway, I must have looked sufficiently meek and penitent, judging from the expression of self-satisfaction on their faces. My mother's mood had changed again. Gone was that veneer of sadness; now if she caught sight of someone she knew, she gave an almost imperceptible nod of greeting, then fixed her gaze proudly ahead, righteous in the knowledge that she was doing her duty by disowning me. The drive lasted about a quarter of an hour, and I can't remember what went through my mind, though doubtless I was praying, to Granny and God impartially. Then the van swung around a corner, and I recognized the road where my aunt lived.

There was the familiar stench of the pond as we drove around it, and I could see the ramshackle houses overlooking the murky waters, the women gossiping, gesticulating, and shrieking across to neighbors from the balconies, and Rosanna, one of my cousins, darting after a cat in the middle of the street. My father was too impatient to wait for a flock of sheep crossing the road. He switched off the engine and ordered us out. I mean, we were only a matter of yards away; it wouldn't have killed him to wait . . . anyway, we climbed down and waited for him to hand us the cases, and with one in each hand made our way toward the house.

On the balconies, the chattering and waving of arms had come to an abrupt halt. The women craned toward us, studying us with great curiosity, doubtless wondering what the three of us were doing, cases in hand. You could see them speculating, discussing us with their neighbors, and trying to find the most plausible explanation for our arrival. Of course it would have been almost simpler if they'd waited to ask my aunt, but they knew she wouldn't divulge the really juicy bits, so why bother?

My aunt was in, and we surged through the door, which was always open, to find her in the kitchen having a cup of coffee. As always she hugged and kissed me warmly, asking how I was. I just shrugged my shoulders. She scolded me for not having been to see her when she was ill, but paused as she saw me hang my head. Seeing that something was wrong, she gave me a little nod of sympathy as if to say, "Don't worry, I'm on your side." Then she turned to my mother and asked how she was. My mother launched into her customary lamentations.

"How do you think I am, saddled with this little trollop? She's taken ten years off my life." My father nodded approvingly, and my aunt said nothing. It was typical that Aunt Vannina never seemed to take sides, in fact always gave the impression of rooting for you. My mother looked pleased, having interpreted Aunt Vannina's silence as a sign of disapproval, an assurance that I would be properly punished. They stayed only long enough for me to take my things into my cousins' room, from where I could hear her next door, weeping out her last instructions on how I should be treated.

As soon as they had gone, my aunt called me into the kitchen and told me not to worry about anything, assuring me that I would be very happy with her. She added that whatever my mother said, she had no intention of treating me like a slave. As she spoke, I longed to confess what her husband had done to me, to confide my fears, but my courage failed me. I was terrified that she too wouldn't believe me, would turn against me like everyone else. In her presence I felt secure and loved once more, and the last thing I wanted was to ruin that feeling with fears that I had doubtless exaggerated and should have put behind me.

Aunt Vannina asked for my side of the story, saying she had heard all sorts of rumors. Someone had told her that I'd been caught by my father half-naked with an old man. So to put the record straight, I told her about the trousers, about Angelina, the party, Nicola, and the little we had actually done. She listened attentively, then told me her story.

"When I was your age, I had a boyfriend too. Like you, we didn't do anything much, but your grandfather got wind of it and beat me to within an inch of my life. As if that wasn't enough, he stopped me going out altogether, and three years later I met your uncle and got married soon after, mainly because I didn't have a chance to look for any Prince Charming, and even if I had my family would have killed me if they'd found out. . . . Don't worry, I'm on your side," she kept saying. "Anyway, we'd better stop chattering and think about your unpacking." She accompanied me to the girls' bedroom, where we did our best to fit sixteen years of my worldly possessions into a couple of empty drawers.

It was ten o'clock, and we had three hours together before my uncle returned. Uncle Vincenzo had perfected the art of appearing to look for work, which somehow he never succeeded in finding. He always had a reason: the job would be too tiring or too badly paid, or the prospective employer would turn out to be arrogant or persnickety or just unsympathetic. Whatever the reason, it meant that yet again Aunt Vannina was forced to make the rounds of the neighbors or her brothers, trying to earn enough to keep the wolf from the door, at least for that day. Something usually did turn up because people knew and admired her; there was a lot of sympathy for her because, as I said earlier, in these parts not even a dog can die without everyone putting their two cents in. On the rare occasions that she couldn't scrape even a little together, she'd go down to the village in search of any odd job so she could buy bread with her self-respect and her dignity intact. The only thing my aunt prided herself on was her reputation for integrity and virtue, though I doubt if anyone would have dared to proposition her. She was good-looking all right, although she had let herself go a bit over the years, with the kind of beauty that neither age nor overwork can destroy, that might fade a bit with the passing years but never vanishes altogether.

Her lustrous black eyes were her most striking feature. She had perfect carriage, and her demeanor, even at the times of greatest humiliation, always had a certain distinction and dignity. She was tall, surprisingly tall given the average height in the village and the fact that her parents and brothers barely topped five feet. She had olive skin flushed with rose (also untypical among this semi-African people) and long black hair, which she always tied back in a ponytail, from which several tendrils escaped to fall over those magnificent dark luminous eyes. Often, exhausted, she would slump into a chair, complaining that life had aged her prematurely, had cheated her of the happiness of knowing her daughters had all they needed like other people's children. Yet even in those moments of despair her eyes betrayed her; they shone with an unerring faith in that same life that had robbed her of what she most cherished, her youth.

Like most children who grew up during the war, she had had a harsh childhood. But hers was harsher than most. Her mother kept a bakery; her father was a fisherman with a passion for antiquities. Aunt Vannina was the youngest of seven, but by no means spoiled or pampered. Mind you, pampering was difficult in those days, though it's a fallacy that childhood unhappiness stems from prosperity, as people around here believe. My father, who was the eldest, was my grandmother's favorite. He was given the family's whole meat ration while his brothers sat there, watching every mouthful. His brothers and sisters seemed not to resent this discrimination, though it must have done even more harm to their souls than to their stomachs. My other uncles and aunts saw nothing strange in his being singled out: he was the eldest and there was a tacit understanding that special treatment was his due. But Aunt Vannina was more sensitive than the others, so she always felt everything more acutely.

There were lots of other privileges for my father besides being given extra food; for instance, he was the only one who was allowed to stay on at school, though Aunt Vannina said that she always had to explain everything to him because he never understood the work, even after he'd been over it a dozen times. She was made to leave school at eleven, so after that she used to sneak off and pore over my father's books at night, a story he teased her with constantly. Aunt

Vannina was forced to give up her studies and then had to endure the sight of her brother cheerfully abandoning his own. She had to stay at home helping her mother with the housework, for which she got no thanks: her mother seemed to have an instinctive dislike of her. No, "instinctive" is the wrong word, because a mother's instinct should be to love her children. What I meant was an irrational, unnatural dislike.

My grandfather on the other hand doted on her; she was the only one he took with him on his fishing trips or when he went to the graveyard to ferret around for old vases and coins. But at home, Grandad counted for no more than a woman normally does in a male-dominated society. His wife held the purse strings and only handed him the odd penny, accompanied by loud strictures on his incompetence.

When she talked about those years, my aunt showed a touch of resentment, a resentment that my father never showed. It was a resentment toward her more fortunate brother who was oblivious to his advantages as the eldest and, above all, as a boy. I loved my grandmother but I still think she was wrong to give him preferential treatment. He was treated like a demigod whose word carried as much weight in his mother's household as it did in his father's family. In a nostalgic mood, my aunt would tell us stories about her youth; she was very sentimental about her past

and seemed deeply attached to it in spite of everything. She told us about the time my father caught her
smoking at the harbor and tried to make her swallow
the cigarette while it was still burning; and the time
my grandfather saw her talking to a boy and felt
obliged to strike her because he was with a friend who
relayed the story to my grandmother. But mostly she
told us stories about the two months she spent at age
twenty with the Ursuline nuns.

One of my great-aunts, who was obsessed with
the church, insisted that Aunt Vannina should become
a nun. So she was made to spend two months in the
convent, very lonely ones since none of the family ever
came to see her. Then in church one day she saw a boy
and convinced herself that she was in love. Who could
blame her? She was twenty and this was the first boy to
make her feel like a woman. They managed to meet a
couple of times before being found out by the mother
superior. Her parents were immediately informed and
came to take her away. They made it their business to
know everything about the boy; they interrogated him
at length and presto, three months later she became
Mrs. Amato. She wasn't too happy about it because by
this time she found out that she wasn't in love, but she
wasn't miserable either; she simply accepted her lot.
She hoped to be able to make up for that lack of love
by having a family of her own.

Rosanna was born a few years later, her firstborn

and favorite, though she did her best to love them equally. My grandmother was not present at the birth but waited a day before coming to see her. The only thing she said when my uncle told her the good news was, "You'd think that between you, you might have managed a son."

Then, when she saw the baby, she exclaimed, "God almighty, what a little monkey!"

First with poor Rosanna, then with Aurelia, my aunt had once again to endure her mother's injustice and dislike, which now embraced the little girls whom she persecuted while spoiling all the other grand-children. Yet when Granny died, Aunt Vannina was the only one to mourn her, the only one who wept at her funeral. To this day, her eyes well up whenever she talks about her mother.

After she had helped me unpack, we made ourselves comfortable in the kitchen and she lit up. Cigarettes were the only luxury she permitted herself and one she was determined not to give up. She smoked with an air of elegant disdain and, I had observed, with much more frequency and relish when my father was around, making no attempt to keep the smoke from blowing right in his face, her secret revenge for that time he had tried to force her to swallow her burning stub. She sat across from me, her legs elegantly crossed, mocking me because I wouldn't smoke. She always offered me a cigarette and was always a bit offended when I smilingly refused it. Perhaps it was because it was the one thing she could give me, her way of trying to get closer to me. I felt we were already pretty close because we'd had similar experiences, but she was shier about expressing her feelings, having always been surrounded by hypocrisy. She had learned to keep her emotions to herself and never quite lost the habit.

I'm sure of all this, not because I'm clairvoyant or anything, but because that morning she found the perfect way to get closer to me and it wasn't a cigarette. We were talking all about what I had done, and she asked what were my dreams and aspirations. I told her that what I most longed for was to be able to wear trousers. She smiled and told me to come with her to her room, where she opened the wardrobe and told me to take off my skirt. Then she slipped a pair of her husband's trousers off the hanger and told me to try them on. I looked at her for a moment, then I did as I was told. The trousers were so baggy that I was almost swimming in them, but she found a belt and buckled it around my waist. Then we burst out laughing because I looked just like a clown. At that moment Aunt Vannina looked at me and said something so sad that I suddenly felt ashamed for having set my sights on something so trivial for so long.

"If only it were always this easy to get what one wants, to find a way of managing."

It was more her expression than the actual words, because her beautiful eyes were suddenly dead. Then they lit up again, and she got up and opened the drawer of the cabinet on her side of the bed and took out a small book bound in brown leather, telling me to read it when I had time. I opened it at once, but she flinched and begged me not to read it in her presence. She said that it had taken all her courage to let me see it at all, that I was the only person who knew it existed, and if I read it when she was around she might not be able to cope with her anxiety and fears and would find herself asking me to return it. I sympathized with her feelings and, hardly able to contain my curiosity, asked if she minded being alone for a while. She said she didn't, so I went to my room, threw myself on the bed, and started to read it right from the beginning.

October 15, 1962

Today I'm twenty and Mom hasn't even been to visit me. I thought Dad might come but there's no sign of him either. The nuns don't know it's my birthday but they wouldn't be interested, so why tell them. Perhaps Mom forgot and that's why she hasn't come. Poor thing, she's got so much else to do. I composed a poem today and wrote it out on toilet paper; Mother Superior sent me in there to clean up and that's when I did it. I'm going to write it out here properly so I don't lose it, and can keep it when I become a nun, and one day, Mother Superior.

> I would like to be a bird
> and fly away
> I would like to be a tiny baby
> suckling my mother's milk
> I would like to be a grownup
> suckling my mother's milk
> I dreamed I was a bird
> on the wing
> I dreamed I was a baby
> suckling my mother's milk
> I dreamed I was a grownup
> suckling my mother's milk
> But then I awoke and found myself here.

I realize this poem is not as beautiful as Leopardi's "Passero Solitario," but that didn't move me a bit and when I read this it brings tears to my eyes.

October 27, 1962

It's been twelve days since I last wrote. I didn't write before for two reasons; firstly because I had no news and secondly because Angelica found the poem which I'd left in the lavatory and she reported me to Mother Superior who said I shouldn't write things like that because it would anger God. Why should it? I scribbled what I felt was true, that is, that I thought no one loved me. Nobody ever comes to see me but the other girls' parents come to see them. Angelica teased me and said I had a complex but I didn't understand what she meant so she explained that it's when a person feels everyone hates them and imagines everyone is against them. I told her that I didn't think that and anyway I really did feel alone and I started crying and she said a strange word to me which I didn't understand. So what! I was dying to ask her what it meant but I didn't want her to take me for an idiot, so I left. But I had wicked thoughts about her and that's a sin. I'm going to bed now because it's late and all the others' lights are out.

November 10, 1962

I haven't written for ages but now I've got tons of news and hardly any time to write because I'm supposed to be asleep like everyone else. It's Sunday and we went to Sant'Angelo for mass. I was sitting with the rest of the girls, then I went up to confession but a boy got in there before me so I hung around until he came out.

He started looking at me so hard that I felt myself blushing and then he laughed, still not taking his eyes off me. Then he stopped me just as I was about to go into the confessional and asked my name. I told him and asked what his was. It was Vincenzo and he's gorgeous; he's got fair hair and hazel eyes and he's quite tall and slim. He said my eyes were the "beautifullest" he'd ever seen and I told him he couldn't say that because it's bad grammar but he said he was entitled to because it was true. He asked me when he could see me again but I told him it wouldn't be allowed because I was going to take my vows. Then he said I wasn't going to become a nun because I was going to marry him. I saw Maria Luisa watching and pointing me out to Assuntina, so Vincenzo and I agreed that he would come to Sant'Angelo every morning at ten thirty and I'd try to be there. When I went back to the others Maria Luisa immediately asked me who I'd been talking to so I said it was my cousin. I can't wait to see Vincenzo again because no one's ever said such lovely things to me. It doesn't feel sinful because I don't want to be a nun anyway, I want to marry and have children like everyone else. I've never kissed anyone and he might tease me because I'm no good at it, actually I don't think he will because I think he already loves me. My knees turned to jelly when he looked at me in that way and he said he wants to marry me and I've got no objections. I must switch off the light now and go to sleep, though it's the last thing I feel like doing. I could write all night and all day but I'd better not, so I'm going to lie down and try to sleep.

November 13, 1962

I'm on cloud nine! Today I kissed Vincenzo, or to be exact he kissed me. I didn't expect him to but it was heaven. I nearly fainted when I saw him because I hadn't been able to get to church before midday so I didn't think he'd still be there. I tried to get there earlier but it took me ages to persuade Mother Superior to let me go with Assuntina to do the shopping. I told Assuntina I was meeting my cousin Vincenzo but she knew I was lying and promised not to spy on me because she has a boyfriend too. So she left me on my own in the church saying she'd come back after she had done the shopping and seen her boyfriend. I thought he would have left because it was so late but he was waiting for me and when he saw me he came rushing up and asked if I was alone, then we left. He told me that he'd been there every day until twelve thirty and when I said I couldn't stay long, he suddenly gave me a big hug and kissed me right on the mouth. I was rooted to the spot and didn't move a muscle because (a) I didn't have the first idea what to do and

91

(b) I thought I was going to faint. Vincenzo said he'd been thinking about me constantly in the last few days and then he asked me if I'd liked him kissing me and when I said yes, he started kissing me again and again. Luckily I don't think he realized I wasn't the world's most experienced kisser or he would have said so. Then he started feeling me up and I told him to stop treating me like some slut he'd picked up off the street. He said I was crazy to say that because he really loved me. He asked if I felt the same and I said no and he said he didn't believe me and I'd got to swear I was telling the truth. I put my hand over my heart but then I cracked up laughing, and he realized I was lying. I love him, although I'm not sure what love is but I do know that I want to marry him, be with him and kiss him for as long as I live.

November 17, 1962

It's a week to the day that I first met Vincenzo. Today, I saw him for the first time in four days. I went out with Assuntina who was meeting her boyfriend and this time she introduced me to him because I'd gone to meet Vincenzo in church but he wasn't there. Her boyfriend is called Lillo, he's twenty-three and an absolute dreamboat. He's a hundred times better looking than Vincenzo and he made a real fuss over me so Assuntina got quite huffy. He told me I was very beautiful and said he wished he'd met me before so he could have gone out with me; he's got a sexy mouth and a dimple when he laughs. Assuntina said they had to leave and Lillo argued with her, saying it was still early and he wanted to stay. In the end she dragged him away saying that it was time I went to meet my boyfriend. So they left me alone but soon Vincenzo arrived and gave me a big kiss. I still like Vincenzo and I like it when we kiss but I find Lillo attractive too, even if he is Assuntina's boyfriend.

November 23, 1962

I think I'm in for it. This morning, that cow Assuntina announced that I couldn't go out with her again because I was such a flirt and I'm going to have to miss my meeting with Vincenzo on Sunday because I've got to be with the nuns so I won't be able to sneak out. I'm disappointed not to see Lillo again. I told Assuntina I hadn't done anything but she said I was a liar. I must see Lillo soon but I don't know how.

November 26, 1962

I dream about your beautiful eyes
And I want to kiss your lips

93

I long to fly away with you to the ends of the earth
Teach me to fly and we'll fly together
It may be a sin
But it is what I desire
It is my heart's desire, dear love.

December 1, 1962

I'm done for. That bitch took my diary and read it and
then told Mother Superior about Vincenzo but of
course she didn't say a word about her and Lillo. So I
told Mother Superior that Assuntina had a boyfriend
too but she scolded me for telling fibs to get myself out
of trouble and I could hear that cow Assuntina snicker-
ing in the background. I told the truth but Mother
Superior said that she would summon my parents and
tell them everything. I'm dreading it. Mom will beat
the hell out of me when she hears. Dear God, please
help!

May 23, 1966

I had a baby yesterday. It's a girl and Vincenzo wants to
call her Ciccina, but I don't. Mom came to see Rosanna today and all she could say was that she was ugly.
I think she's very pretty because she's got blue eyes
and a few tufts of blond hair. Vincenzo said that Mom

told him Antonio had a boy and she'd hoped I would too but I'm not my brother. Perhaps she didn't tell me because she knew it would make me cross. Well, I'm pleased she's a girl and I'm mad about her.

April 7, 1967

Rosanna is growing fast and I don't have time to write in my diary. Vincenzo can't find a job and Rosanna is hungry all the time. I take her along when I go to people's homes to give them injections and sometimes the ladies give her cakes because she's so adorable. She chatters away now but the very first word she said was "Mama." I was so moved I was almost in tears. Mom says that she's cross-eyed but I've looked carefully and I don't think she is, her eyes are lovely and straight. They're the same color as Vincenzo's now and her hair is getting darker.

May 22, 1967

Rosanna is one today. I'd love to give her something but we're desperately hard up. I told Vincenzo, but he called me a moron because there's hardly enough to feed us but he's a fine one to talk, he finds enough for drink even though he knows that Rosanna has scarcely a rag on her back. He never gives her a hug or a kiss these days. When it comes to that he never kisses me either except when he's trying to get me into bed and then he starts slobbering all over me and makes me feel sick because his breath stinks of wine.

July 17, 1968

Today was a nightmare. Aunt Concetta told me there was a lady in the village who was looking for a maid, so I went to the house and who should open the door but Assuntina. Their house is right in the center, overlooking the piazza, it took my breath away, and it's all so clean and tidy. When she first saw me she looked as if she couldn't believe her eyes, but then she gave me a big hug. She said that she and Lillo had got married and they were comfortably off because he was an accountant at the bank but he wasn't back yet. They have two children who were asleep. She didn't say a word about housework because we were so busy chatting, then it started to get late and I said I must go but she begged me to stay for supper and I told her I'd have to ask my husband. So she suggested I ring him but we don't have a phone so she said they would gladly take me home at the end of the evening. She was determined that Lillo and I should see each other. And then, when he came in, Assuntina ordered me to start cleaning immediately if I wanted the money. I felt like telling her to do it herself with her clean, dainty hands but then I remembered how hungry Rosanna was, so I got the cloth and bleach and made a start on the floor. He was even more handsome than I remembered; he was wearing a lovely suit and looked a real gentleman. He gave her a peck on the cheek and she told him who I was but he didn't remember me until he looked more closely and recognized my eyes. He said I was still beautiful and Assuntina was furious and told me to carry on cleaning and she told Lillo I was married and dirt poor. Lillo said Rosanna looked really sweet and took no notice of Assuntina, in fact he seemed quite embarrassed by the way she was carrying on. But I noticed he was looking at me strangely as though he felt sorry for me. I think he wanted me to stop slaving for them and leave but I couldn't go home empty handed. He asked me to stay for dinner too but I said no. So I went on cleaning while they had dinner, and I heard him being cross with her for treating me like that, and it was really odd because they were talking in Italian the whole time and didn't lapse into Sicilian even when the conversation got heated. When I had finished, Lillo didn't let Assuntina give me the money but insisted on paying me himself. He asked me to forgive her and pressed a wad of bills into my hand. I said it was too much but he said I'd really earned it and added that I could always go to him for help. I was too choked up to speak. I left without saying good-bye to Assuntina. I really appreciated Lillo's kindness and he'd looked so handsome. I hid the money from Vincenzo, otherwise he'll ask endless questions and accuse me of being a tramp and grab all of it. I wish I was a lady so Lillo would like me more.

Why am I so poor? It's not fair.
Why should Rosanna go hungry?
And why did Lillo have to see me like that?
I wish I was a lady
A lady with money
A lady with fine clothes
A lady with jewelry
Quite simply a lady.

September 15, 1969

I'm no better than a prostitute. I'm disgusting. I went to see Lillo at the bank today because I really needed some money, though I know that's not why I really went. I put on my prettiest dress and washed my hair and made myself up, and when I put my hat on I felt a real lady. He couldn't take his eyes off me and told me I looked stunning. He took me to the café across the road and bought me a drink; everyone in there knew him and I think they stared at me because I looked so ladylike. We sat very close, with our heads together and our mouths almost touching and I found myself wondering about how his kisses would taste. We left the café and he drove to the harbor so we could talk in peace. I told him I needed his help and he said he'd do whatever he could. Before I realized what was happening, we were gazing into each other's eyes and kissing passionately. I'm going to see him again tomorrow morning if Enza can baby-sit for me. His lips tasted even better than I'd imagined even if he did have a martini in the bar. When I think of Vincenzo he always has foul breath, whether he's been near a bottle or not.

September 17, 1969

Now I really do feel like a whore. Yesterday I met Lillo and he drove me to the house of a friend of his. I didn't want to do it. I mean I hadn't meant to, but when he started caressing me I didn't tell him to stop because he was so tender and respectful. What we did was beautiful even though it was wrong. He made me feel so good though it's horrible with Vincenzo. Lillo asked me when we could see each other again but I didn't know. I said we could meet when I went to the bank but he said that it was too risky. I think he feels guilty. Anyway, in the end we agreed that whenever I had the chance, I would meet him over at the café during his break at eleven. I can't wait to see him and I don't feel in the least bit guilty.

October 6, 1969

I don't know what to do because I think I'm pregnant and I haven't slept with Vincenzo for ages so it must be Lillo's baby. We only made love that one time but God has seen fit to punish me for that one moment of happiness. I'm frightened to go to the doctor because I know what he'll say and I'm frantic because I haven't a clue what to do.

January 1, 1971

Here we are at the beginning of a new year again. Aurelia isn't well. I think she may have a temperature and I ought to call the doctor. I haven't seen Lillo for months and I must, to give him news of our daughter. Vincenzo can't stand Aurelia and when she cries he starts drinking and then hits her. Thank God I'm there to cuddle her in my arms. I haven't told Vincenzo she's not his but I think he guesses because he always treats her so badly. Perhaps it's because she doesn't look a bit like him. I've started seeing Lillo again and he's become unbearable. He's always saying horrible things and asking what I do with Vincenzo in bed. I've told him a hundred times that I haven't slept with him for a year, except for that one time so he'd think the baby was his, but he won't listen and says if I can be unfaithful to my husband with him I could just as easily be unfaithful to him with my husband or with anyone else for that matter. I often say that he still makes love to Assuntina but he just says that it's his duty as a man; well if that's the case then I'll be a man any day!

May 22, 1973

My eyes are so blurry with tears I can barely see this page. Life makes me sick. Vincenzo has left and I'm done for. I can't go on living here anymore. Today he raped me and beat the living daylights out of me. What should I do? I don't understand anything anymore. Assuntina came to the house and told Vincenzo that Lillo is Aurelia's father and she couldn't hold on to him because he had made up his mind to leave her for me. I begged him not to leave Assuntina because I couldn't leave Vincenzo and Rosanna to be with him and Aurelia. Rosanna's my daughter too and I love her, though not as much as Aurelia. I treat Rosanna better so that no one suspects anything and sometimes when I see Rosanna wanting to hit Aurelia, I'm tempted to give her a good spanking. Vincenzo gave me one and then tore my clothes off and threw me on the bed and then undid his trousers. I thought I would throw up but every time I told him to stop he said that I was a good-for-nothing whore and that's how I deserved to be treated. I could hear Rosanna crying outside the door, asking to be let in. Luckily it was closed so she couldn't see the horrible things he was doing which would have made her cry even more. Then he took all the money from the drawer and stomped out. He's gone for more wine and when he gets home he'll be drunk again, and he'll hit me some more and say those horrible things. He kept on asking how much I'd made on the game. And he said I was a fool and if I had half a brain in my head I'd charge more, he said I wasn't even a good lay. I wanted to tell him that I hadn't "been laid" as he put it, that when Lillo and I made love he said it was the most beautiful experience of his life. I am scared he'll do some harm to Aurelia because he seems to have gone crazy.

By this time my eyes were full of tears. I was just about to turn over the page when Aunt Vannina burst in, crying, "Quick, quick, Annetta, hide it. Vincenzo's coming. Hurry." I shot up, and pushed it under the mattress as quickly as I could. A second later there he was in my room.

"So there you are. What time did you get here?"

Aunt Vannina answered as he came up to kiss me. His touch repelled me, but there was nothing I could do to dodge his horrible lips on my cheek and his revolting breath. Aunt Vannina called us to the table because lunch was ready. I had been so engrossed in that exciting, moving discovery of my aunt as she really was that I hadn't noticed it was lunchtime already. As she served the overcooked steaming pasta from the bowl, she looked at me searchingly, trying to read my reaction in my eyes. But at that moment there was no way I could have explained what I felt because I didn't know myself. I had read that diary with my heart, and it was with my heart that I could judge it — just then I felt incapable of passing judgment on her. All I wanted was for lunch to be over and for him to go off for his siesta, as people do around here, so I could pick up where I had left off.

But as I waited I had to endure his barrage of nosy questions, which he invariably answered himself with some vulgar remark like, "Well, well, aren't you a big girl now?" While I had to go on eating and pretend that I hadn't picked up on the sexual innuendo, his words, "We'll continue another time," were ringing in my head. It was another time now. It could be today, perhaps, or tomorrow . . . this was his chance to finish what he had started all those years ago. Who was there to protect me? My aunt? Well, she hadn't been able to protect herself so she couldn't help. I was alone and at his mercy, and he knew it. Never again would Granny be there to save me. The moment lunch was over I excused myself from the table and went to my room. I took the diary from under the mattress and began to read as if my life depended on it, partly in an attempt to block out the fear and helplessness that gripped me every time I imagined him saying, "We'll continue another time."

May 23, 1973

Thank God I've got this diary to write down my thoughts and feelings or I'd have gone mad. Vincenzo came in well past one last night and I pretended to be asleep. As he was undressing he kept repeating that he'd married a slut who was a lousy lay to boot. I could tell he'd been with a real slut, someone who gets paid to do it and he's paid her with money I'd earned. Then he fell into bed and I knew he wasn't asleep because I could hear him crying; even when he cries he's disgusting because he wipes his nose with the back of his hand and then smears it on the sheet. It's not the first time, he cries every time he's plastered. Once I tried to comfort him because I couldn't understand why he was crying and then he burst out laughing, broke down in tears a moment later and then slapped me hard on the face. Next day he said he didn't remember a thing about it so now I don't even bother to tell him when he behaves like that. This time, I pretended to be asleep but he kept tweaking my arm and trying to shake me awake. I went to see Mom this morning because I am sure he's going to do something awful to

Aurelia. I asked if I could stay there and I was in such a state that I burst into tears myself. Mom made me go back because she said Vincenzo was my husband and I'd made my choice. Well, that was a great help! I haven't seen Lillo because I can't go out anymore, not even to work. What sort of life is this?

July 7, 1974

Mom's dead and they're deciding who the house should go to because she didn't leave a will. I want my mommy . . .

December 16, 1974

Now Dad's gone too, we all thought he would because he'd been ill ever since Mom died and was always crying and calling for her. I am alone now, Mom and Dad have left me and I'm all alone. Vincenzo says he's going off to Switzerland to look for work. He says that we'll starve if we stay here but he knows very well that thanks to me he's never been in danger of starving. I'm glad he's going because then I won't be frightened anymore.

December 20, 1974

Vincenzo has told me that he's leaving for Switzerland with a friend at the end of the month. He can go today for all I care, in fact he'd be doing me a favor. The problem is that he wants to take Rosanna with him so she can see a specialist there and have an operation after he's succeeded in getting the money together, because those operations cost a fortune. Mom always said she was cross-eyed but I didn't want to believe it. I started noticing her eyes looked funny after Aurelia was born. I don't want Vincenzo to take her away.

January 4, 1975

Vincenzo left for Switzerland yesterday and took Rosanna with him without my knowing. I had gone to clean for Miss Vincenti and when I got back Rosanna was gone and Aurelia was all alone. She said Vincenzo's friend came to pick him up and Vincenzo told Rosanna to collect her things and go with them. Rosanna started crying and saying she didn't want to leave without me but he slapped her and forced her into the car. They left Aurelia alone in the house and Vincenzo knows she hates that. I must go to see Lillo in the bank. He and Assuntina are getting divorced, she told me when she came here and kicked up such a stink. What should I say to him when we meet? It's been so long since I last saw him.

June 15, 1975

Today I got a letter from Vincenzo, the first in all these months. He says he's bought a car and that he went to see a doctor who told him the operation is very expensive so we can't afford it. They might come home for Christmas but he's not certain because he's got a lot of work. I see Lillo every day and now he picks us up from home because he doesn't give a damn about what people think, but I know what's going on in those heads of theirs and when Vincenzo comes back someone's bound to spill the beans. Lillo is always saying that he'll marry me when his divorce comes through but Assuntina never leaves him alone, she phones him at the bank day after day and she won't allow him to see the children. I would like to leave this place and be alone, without Lillo or anyone.

November 23, 1975

Lillo came over today to tell me that he's made up with Assuntina and they're back together again. But he said that we could still see each other, though not every day, but I told him to forget it. I am glad that he's with Assuntina, though now I'm all alone again.

December 17, 1975

Lillo came looking for me today. I've told him not to, but he turns up anyway because he says he's fed up with Assuntina who is pregnant and always complaining. He wanted to make love but I refused, then he said he was desperate because he hadn't done it for ages. So who made Assuntina pregnant then, the Holy Ghost? Then I felt sorry for him, so we did it. It's Christmas soon and Vincenzo will be home.

The diary ended here and I knew I'd have to wait until Vincenzo had gone out to hear the rest. I was longing to find out what had become of Lillo, how Aunt Vannina had managed to go on living with Vincenzo, and what she felt now. I had to hold out for longer than I'd expected, because they both disappeared to the village and didn't get back till nearly eight. We had supper together, then he went off for his usual session in the bar and at last I got a chance to talk to her. I didn't know where to begin, but my aunt helped me out by speaking first.

"Have you finished it?"

"Yes, I have . . . I've been longing to ask you how things ended with you and that man."

"You mean Lillo? Oh, nothing much. I see him around the village from time to time."

"But, Aunt Vannina, what about later, after your diary ended?"

And so, after some hesitation, my aunt told me the rest of her story. Lillo stayed with his wife and could be seen every Sunday morning walking to mass and every Sunday evening as they strolled arm in arm in the piazza, followed by their three children. As for my uncle, he did come back that Christmas and their lives went on as before. Every now and again he needled her about her lapse, blithely ignoring what was common knowledge, thanks to his friend, that while he was in Switzerland he'd shacked up with a woman whose morals weren't just dubious, they were nonexistent. By some miracle no one blabbed about Lillo's visits. I think it was because people loved and respected my aunt so much.

And what did she hope for now, I asked. She just shrugged her shoulders. What struck me as most ironic in the whole story was that she got pregnant the only time she really enjoyed making love, while all the other times, and God knows there were enough of them, nothing had happened. Perhaps she didn't get punished by pregnancy all those times because the act was punishment enough. So now she hoped for nothing, or

wouldn't allow herself to, so as to avoid further disap-
pointments. Here, she looked at me and asked what I
thought of her now. I found I couldn't speak, but we fell
into each other's arms and she cried a bit. By this time I
was bursting to tell her what her husband had done to
me, and the more I told myself that it wasn't fair to her,
the more I felt I had to. Finally I just blurted it out,
avoiding any details, simply giving a brief version of the
events. She didn't show any surprise, and I was relieved
that she didn't pretend. Then she murmured, "That
filthy pig . . ." and turned to me, saying it wasn't safe for
me to be in the house. I think it was this that finally
triggered the most important decision of her life: she
would leave home, taking the children and nothing else
except a little money and a handful of new dreams. As
always her eyes shone with intensity as she described
her plans. And what about me? Well, naturally, she
would take me with her, she said.

The next day she and I went to see Lillo at what
she called "his bank," to tell him what we'd decided.
My aunt was a bundle of nerves, though she did her
best to hide it. I could tell, because she had had at least
ten cigarettes since eight o'clock and it was now barely
ten. However, she was determined to go through with
it. Her voice was steady, and she maintained an appearance of calm, but as soon as we found ourselves in
front of the glass doors to the bank, she went all shaky
and said we must go home, that there had to be some

less drastic course of action. I was a bit thrown by her
sudden change of mood and the new plan, but I
thought it must be because it was so terribly important
to her, especially in view of the life she'd led.

I could see why she was in such a state when Lillo
came out to speak to her and I saw him for the first
time. He really was handsome and quite young-
looking. He had a lovely face and a sensual mouth.
When he saw Aunt Vannina he rushed to the door to
meet her and asked her to wait for a minute. Then he
was back, saying he was off the hook for an hour, so we
all went to the bar and he asked her who I was and why
she'd brought me along. She just said I was her niece,
and then she began telling him what she'd decided,
but now I noticed she got all humble and hesitant. I
soon saw why. Lillo lost his temper and started yelling
like a madman, and my aunt's attempts at calming him
down were useless — he just wouldn't hear reason.
Half a dozen heads swiveled in our direction, and it
was clear he wanted to leave but he couldn't because
of me. He told me to get out, while my aunt pleaded
with me to stay. She looked terrified, and he kept
shouting at me to go while she was begging me to stay.
Then he slapped her across the face, so she gave in
and told me to do as he said, saying she'd be home in a
while.

I had no idea what to do. I knew she shouldn't be
left alone with that lunatic. While I was dithering he

bellowed, "Well, what are you waiting for, girl? Go on, scat!" And so I went. When I got home, I waited for her for hours, while Uncle Vincenzo subjected me to a Gestapo-like interrogation as to her whereabouts. She still wasn't back five hours later, and my cousins were crying all that time and I was frantic with worry, imagining her lying dead somewhere. The clock struck eleven, and there was still no sign of her. The girls had been put to bed, though my uncle had given Aurelia a couple of sharp slaps on the face to make her go to sleep. The danger I was in, being alone with him, hadn't dawned on me yet.

Ever the optimist, I thought he would be too worried about his wife's disappearance to contemplate making any moves on me. Indeed, he sat around looking as if he couldn't stir from his gloom. But at midnight his mood changed abruptly.

"All right, come on, Annetta. You don't want to be all by yourself tonight."

"But I won't be by myself. I'm in with Rosanna and Aurelia," I said hurriedly.

"You know what I mean. Your parents aren't here, are they, so you'll sleep with me in my room tonight."

"No, really, Uncle Vincenzo, don't worry. I'm not in the least bit frightened," I said, doing my best to sound nonchalant.

"Come on now, don't be silly. My mind's made up."

"But Uncle, the girls can't be left on their own."

"Oh, forget about them. You're sleeping with me and that's final."

With that, he took me by the arm and dragged me into the bedroom. It hurt so much that I forgot to be afraid until he began to undress. "You can't sleep with all your clothes on," he said. "Come on, let's have a look at you."

He was drunk of course, and he looked completely demented. I said I had no intention of staying with him, and then he stood up and dropped his trousers before my very eyes. He forced me onto my knees in front of him and yanked me by my hair toward his penis. I screamed bloody murder, while he tugged so hard I thought he'd wrench my hair out at the roots. At this moment Rosanna stumbled sleepily in at the door, which he hadn't even had the decency to close, and when she saw us like that, a look of relief crossed her face, and she whispered, "Don't worry, Annetta. Daddy's just giving you a drink of milk."

It took a while for the penny to drop, while he just laughed and said, "The milk's tasty, Annetta. Go on, try it."

Then all of a sudden the truth socked me between the eyes, and I bolted from the house. I fled in my nightdress and slippers, along the unpaved roads and pathways. I felt the soft grass underfoot and the foul pond stank in my nostrils. There were scarcely any cars at that time of night, and drunks asked where I was going while passersby gawked at me with disbelief and curiosity. I hated my aunt for not having come back that evening and for having allowed that animal to use his own daughters for his perverted games.

I had no idea where to turn. I thought about home, but it was my home no longer, if it ever had been. A car came up beside me, and it was *him*, blasting his horn. He shouted at me to halt and get in the car with him, pointing out that I had nowhere else to go. My parents wouldn't believe my story, and they wouldn't have me back. He was right, of course, but I'd have done anything not to go back with *him*, to that house. As he tried to block my escape with the car, I suddenly remembered that Angelina Carasotti lived nearby. I broke into a run again, just managing to keep ahead, and finally dashed into an alley that was too narrow for him to drive down. But he caught sight of me and got out of the car. I reached Angelina's front door and barely had time to ring their doorbell before he was there beside me. I screamed up to Angelina while he kicked me and tried to drag me away. Mr. Carasotti flung open a window, demanding to know what was going on.

"It's me, Annetta," I shouted. "Help me, An-gelina, he's going to kill me, help, help!"

I was frantic, yelling as loud as I could, when someone shouted down: "Leave her alone. Get away from her. Get away right this minute, or I'll send for the police."

"Mind your own frigging business, or I'll clobber you too," came the reply.

Mr. Carasotti yelled to his wife and told her to telephone the police, then ran down to help me. I could hear the fright in her voice as she asked what was happening. Her husband ran down in his dressing gown, and my uncle let go of me, looking around for something to hit him with. He found an iron bar lying on the ground and stood in wait by the front door. Terrified, I screamed a warning to Mr. Carasotti: "Watch out, watch out!" and I ran off to get help.

The streets were deserted except for the odd stray dog. At last I heard a car and stood in the middle of the road, waving my arms to flag it down. "Help," I cried. "Help! They're going to kill each other. Quick!" There were three of them, and they leaped out to chase my uncle, who was hot in pursuit of Mr. Car-asotti, brandishing the iron bar. He had already hit him on the shoulder, shouting, "Go on, run, you bas-tard!"

Mrs. Carasotti and Angelina were hanging over the balcony, screaming for help. At last the police

115

arrived, as the three men struggled with my uncle, who was thrashing around and cursing. We all trooped down to the police station, and they wanted to know everything — my name, who my parents were, why I was living with my uncle, and where my aunt was. Then despite my pleas and the reassurances of Angelina and her parents, they said my parents must be contacted.

Mr. Carasotti and his wife were really kind, pressing me to stay with them if there were any problems, and saying I must make a formal accusation against my uncle for attempted rape. They insisted that he must be punished because of the appalling nature of his crimes. Then my parents arrived, and I immediately spotted that familiar look of scepticism in my father's face. I could see he thought I was about to bring yet more shame upon the family and could barely keep his hands from my throat. My mother knew no such restraint. She fell on me like a fury, clawing and scratching. She even sank her teeth into me like a she-wolf. But Mr. Carasotti pulled her off and she had to stop gnawing at her goodly repast. She demanded to know what right he had to stick his nose into other people's business. Wasn't he satisfied with what his daughter had done to me, wasn't it enough that she'd turned her angelic little girl into a dirty slut. Mr. Carasotti shut her up by saying that no one had the right to hit people, least of all their own children, and he wouldn't allow her to lay a finger on me ever again.

Meanwhile, Angelina and her mother had taken me aside and were stroking my hair and whispering soothingly. That night, and many nights afterward, I slept at their house. They treated me very well, almost as if I was Angelina's younger sister, and Angelina generously lent me her clothes and took me out with her. That was a happy month for me, because for once I felt like an ordinary, balanced person living a normal life. But I didn't expect this Eden to last.

I ran into Nicola again, and we started seeing each other regularly. I found I really liked him. He had an attractive mind and felt strongly that men and women should be equal. He was so sweet too, overwhelming me with affection and thoughtfulness, and I soon began to think of him as the Prince Charming I had never sought in the past. At this point my parents remembered they had a daughter and took me back into the fold, doubtless with the aim of salvaging what remained of my honor after my stay in the Carasotti household. They made an awful fuss about Nicola, and people began to speculate about my parents sorting everything out and marrying me off to some father figure of a husband if Nicola left me in the lurch. My father made a thorough investigation into his family and even went to see them behind my back to "clarify the situation." To his delight they were just as stick-in-the-mud as he was and eager to assure him that Nicola's intentions were strictly honorable.

A year later Nicola and I were joined in holy matrimony — or is it so holy? I'm not sure — and embarked on creating a new, if not always entirely welcome, family. Many years have passed since then, and I've seen a positive revolution in the attitudes here. Now parents seem to be much less strict, and girls are allowed out when they like. They nearly all go to school, and some even go on to the university, but good girls don't wear trousers and I never achieved my dream of wearing them.

I said as much to Aunt Vannina when she came to visit the other day (she eloped with Lillo, but they split up, and now her lover is a rich, married doctor with a brood of children and, guess what, Uncle Vincenzo is sponging off the Malaspinas in Caltanissetta) — anyway, I told her, and she said, "But Annetta, why did you get married?"

"Well, I might be able to change one mind, but I can't change them all," I replied.

Then she was silent, and I reminded her of the time she dressed me up in Uncle Vincenzo's trousers, and we laughed until we cried.